A Stand of Trees

A STAND OF TREES

ANNE WARNER

Library of Congress Control Number:		2015912794
ISBN:	Hardcover	978-1-5035-9361-9
	Softcover	978-1-5035-9360-2
	eBook	978-1-5035-9430-2

Print information available on the last page.

Rev. date: 08/11/2015

To order additional copies of this book, contact:
Xlibris
1-888-795-4274
www.Xlibris.com
Orders@Xlibris.com
720990

Dedication

This book is dedicated to my parent's and my daughter, with love.

CHAPTER 1

The sun set over the mountain range, casting a soft golden glow over the fields along the road towards his home, as Joachim Cordero rode slowly down the dirt road seeing it in the distance. Stopping, he admired the herd of horses grazing in the pasture, just ahead. All at once, one of the fine stallions broke loose and ran, causing several of the others to follow it across the field. It had taken off at a brisk pace, galloping down the split log fence line, kicking up dust as it went. He laughed, thinking it must be one of those he and his nephew, Jean had brought over from the northern valley, Full of the gusto the breed was so well known for. The herd of twenty, which had been in demand since acquiring the last few horses purchased from the auction in the next county, had been set out to graze that morning by his hands, who expertly maintained them. Joachim, himself, having grown up in the horse country of Portugal was considered an expert, taught by his father, who performed for the royal courts on his well trained stallion. Stomping nervously, his horse lifted its head and neighed loudly. Judging the distance, he kicked his horse once and took off at a full gallop down the dirt road after them. Catching up to the small herd of horses, he took the fence in one leap, landing with a thud, hooves hitting the rock hard dirt. Cordero leaned back in his saddle, breathing heavily, reaching for his hat he wiped the dirt and moisture from his eyes, replacing it at a jaunt. Swinging his horse around, he looked back towards the mountain range, now shadowed in the late afternoon sun. Then, letting out a whistle, he walked his horse to fence, sliding off it easily. Taking the reins, he tied a loop around the post, patting the horse's neck. La Pueda del Sol, the low slung mountain range of the most distinctive rock and shale coloring lay to the east. Sun reflected off the mountains, casting a bright yellow glow around the small valley, surrounded by wooded foothills. Scattered among the fields, were the ranches which dotted the landscape along with the large plots of land they used for grazing. Cordero, having made his way over from the coast, followed the footsteps of those who had begun the original trail to the east. He, having traveled into the western low coastal valleys from across the deserts of the Mexican and Arizona Territories, only to find his home.

Looking out towards the foothills, he could see the rooftop of the log cabin built by he and his nephew, Jean Leandre, twenty years ago. He kicked his horse into a trot and made his way over the plowed field. Stopping, he sighed softly and whispered, "Ah-hah, there they stand, full of golden glory." He laughed, looking up at the row of seven, large stately trees lining the dirt road.

"Why, they must be at least forty feet by now," he thought to himself. "I wonder who planted them so daringly in such wild and untamed territory?" He paused, smiling to himself. "A conquistador?" He laughed lightly. "Most probably an ancestor," he sighed. "Surely must be half a century old, by now, judging by the looks of them." He stopped, looking up and saw, just then, a small golden leaf, bright against the green foliage, curl and wind its way down to the ground, falling in a long, slow dance, blowing gently over the ground to his feet. How very like life itself, he thought, coming full circle to the earth once again. His tired and dusty boots hit the ground and he walked his horse the rest of the way to the corral to graze for the night. Glancing back at the first large tree, he remembered that day. They had come from the river, fully fed by it and refreshed from a long three day ride. Jean, who had been hunting just over the ridge, had looked out over the small valley, spotting the tell tale sign, so talked about from his Grand Uncle Arman's journal. Joachim, along with his nephew and Quinn had raced to the location, sure to find great treasures, they had laughed. Quinn, he'd said, "Come see this..." What a friend he ended being all these years, he thought. One of the biggest cattle ranchers in the west now, he had loved the mystique of the land as much as he did. And then, the surprise. The symbol still visible even now, twenty years later, had been etched deep into its surface of the large oak tree by Arman Ortero Codero with his initials still seen above the carved emblem. The beginning and the ending all recorded in that one symbol... the element for gold. From that day forward, a family mystery had began to unravel, one from over twenty five hundred years ago. And in all places, the mountains of the west... America.

It had begun, quite innocently, when Joachim, just a young man at fourteen had found out just how valuable his skills were needed as horseman, working with the families's rich stash of horses. A claim to the expertise having come from the exclusive and private training given to him by his father, Diego Rafael Cordero. A third generation performer and breeder of the rare and beautiful stallions, known as Andalusian, a line originally bred from the knight's horses of the king of Spain in the early sixteen hundreds.

Having trained his son since he was seven years old to ride the high stepping horses, Diego had become known in the royal courts for his style and expert showmanship. With awe inspiring precision and ability to perform maneuvers in strict formations, the stallions performed to sell out crowds. The fertile lands between the coastal cities, boasted of the estates of both his father, Antone Mercado and his uncle Arman Ortero, the Cordero brothers.

The Cordero estates were often sought after by many who traveled far and wide to make purchases from the wide variety of cattle, mostly longhorn steers and the pure bred horses. He had just finished assisting with one such performance with his father, Diego, when an opportunity became known to them from an important businessman hailing from the city of Lisbon. He had been seeking a map-maker, he'd said. After asking several local businessmen who may know of a cartographer, his Uncle Arman had been recommended. The man had made his way to the Cordero estate to see what, of the thirty head of horses could be purchased, hoping to meet the man, known for his neat and valuable skills as a mapper. Arman, having been trained in the Portuguese manner of cartography was quickly signed on, happy to have the opportunity to use his skills in what seemed a great adventure, a trip to the America's. A ship had been secured and passage for several horses and the passengers were made ready to leave in two weeks time. Meeting up with the businessman once more, he was given his papers for travel and orders to meet up at the port in two weeks, with one well trained horse of his own and his belongings, neatly packed into two leather saddlebags. The trip would be for three months, as explained by the businessman, to help find and secure lands for establishing a cattle ranch. Seeking out his nephew, Diego, Arman spoke to him quietly about what it all entailed. They smiled, suddenly, as a thought that came to them both. They gave each other secret knowing looks and called out to the young son, Joachim to go and collect his grandfather at once, telling him they had something of importance to speak to him about. Antone, who had been an explorer and collector of antiquities for many years, traveled throughout Europe for weeks at a time exploring. He had just returned from a trip to the east, when his young grandson, raced to the house, just three fields down the lane. Reaching the door, he leaned over, catching his breath. Knocking loudly once, then twice more on the large wooden door, he could hear footsteps coming towards him and his grandmother's voice calling out to see who it was. A moment later, she had ushered him, with a hug and a gesture to the kitchen, where she immediately ordered a large glass of milk for the boy. Calling out to her husband to join them in the warmly lit room, she placed a plate of cookies on the table, smiling at her grandson. He quickly grabbed two, placing one into his front pocket and swallowing the other almost in one bite.

Looking up at his grandfather as he strode into the room, he jumped up. "Sir, Grandfather, my father and Uncle Arman insist you come at once, Sir," he said loudly. "They have something to tell you about an upcoming trip abroad." He nodded at him, smiling. "Well, let's take our leave then, shall we?" He said. Turning to his wife, "Bundle up some of those for the men.", he said, smiling at her. "I'll go see what the fuss is all about." Giving her a tender look, he took the cookies she handed him and hugged her close. "Let's go, young man." pointing to the door. "Did you bring your horse?" He asked Joachim. "No, grandfather, I ran all the way." He laughed, and guided his grandson to the barn, where he nodded to the groomsman to bring him his prized stallion.

Swinging his leg over the saddle, he leaned over and held out his hand, "Here, Joachim, let me help you up." Pulling him up on back of the saddle, he said. "Old boy, he is ready for a ride, probably thinks I've forgotten all about him having been gone these past three weeks." He grabbed onto the back of the saddle as his grandfather kicked the horse into a gallop. A rare beauty, the grey stallion with its long black mane had been much sought after by breeders all throughout Europe for its desirable linage and knowing it's owner well trusted his every move. The distinctive markings and high arched neck of the stallion making it one of the favorites for breeding in the area. Looking up, the men, heard the thud of horse hooves and stepped out onto the porch, looking up the dusty road between the homes.

Seeing his brother, racing towards them, Arman held up his arms waving, laughing at them. "Yes, yes, please show us your standard, by all means", he called out. They rode up and stopped with a flourish. Antone gave his grandson a hand down of the back of the horse and then slid off his horse. handing him the reins, nodding to him to tie it to the trees next to the house. Grabbing another cookie out of his pocket, he did as he was told. The men talked quietly, stepping into the house, where they stood, looking at each other seriously. "Let's sit for a while and discuss the possibilities," said Arman. "What do you think, Antone?" He asked. "Might it be a profitable venture for us, these America's?" He looked at him over the papers he had been handed, a bit skeptical. Finally, putting away his eyeglasses, he sighed. "If there is one thing we now know, we do have all the best of the breed secured." "We could explore the west, I think, yes, yes, of course, we could." He paused. "What of this man, do you think he's capable of making the trip a success?" He looked over to Arman with a questioning look on his face.

Arman, sighed, pulling a long leather tube from the floor by his side and placed it on the table, unhooking the lid. He peered inside, motioning with his hand to come, sit down by him as he unrolled the papers that had been inside. Holding it down so they could see, he showed them the long straight lines drawn indicating the longitude and latitude of the coastal areas between the continents. Looking at his brother, Antone, the eldest by five years, he said. "We have much to consider... the estates, the herds, and of course the family." Diego stepped in, after listening quietly, giving his father a stern look, shaking his head. "No, I won't go, father, not this time." He paused. "But do send Uncle Arman with some of the family's horses to sell." Tapping the map, he said. "Have him secure some land for us there." He paused. "I am already on the circuit for this year or I would have liked to go on this great adventure with you." Arman, sighed, looking at his brother and nodded. "It's time, then."

"I'll leave the week after next." He looked at them. "I can make arrangements for at least a half dozen more horses to take," He said, looking around. "Where is that boy?" of his nephew, Joachim, Diego asked. "He's out on the porch." Nodding, he stepped back and pulled the wooden table over by a few feet. Arman then reached down and pulled the latch on the door to the cellar below. "I have room for just a few trinkets to sell, Antone", he said. Kneeling, he pulled a heavy box out of the recess in the wooden floor and heaved it onto the table. Antone stepped forward and twisted the lock and it opened, revealing packages neatly wrapped in soft cloth. He took one and handed it to Arman, reminding him to keep it safe. He looked at it carefully, not even opening it. He withdrew another, a heavier one which he opened, letting them see what was inside. The two men looked, surprised at the contents. Giving each other a look of warning look, Antone quickly wrapped it up again and put it aside with two others. "I'll speak with the captain, Father and see that all will remain secure as Arman travels", Diego said. "I think it will be a grand adventure one day, for us all to go see this great land they call the America's." He laughed. "Better for us to be landowners, than not, don't you agree?" He asked. They laughed, along with him. Arman gave Joachim a tap on the shoulder, while glancing at the clock on the wall, Diego suggested it was late and he'd better get his son home before his mother went in search of them. "I say, Father, I am anxious to hear of your trip," He said. "We'll be over this way again on the morrow, perhaps we can speak then," He nodded, glancing over at the tired face of his son, nodding sleepily by the fire. "Let us go son, your mother is waiting." Joachim stood up shaking hands with his grandfather and walked to the door. The evening air was chilly and it woke him as they rode silent in the carriage brought by his father to his Uncle Arman's home. The moon shone bright as they rode the five miles up the road. The lights from the windows were lit by the glow of the fireplace and smoke tendrils curled up against the night sky. Their home, one of the three largest in the valley, had been built of the rough hewn stone found only in the quarries in the nearby mountains. A deep rich gray in color, it boasted a large carved pine door, with the family crest carved within it. Diego's parcel had included the large creek which ran alongside the property, which consisted of ten acres, mostly for the grazing of cattle. All seemed quiet this evening, the stock grazing in the fields nearby and the horse herd secured in the back pasture. Quiet now, he sensed something had changed and he made a mental note to speak to his father about the sale of the horses, all of sudden reluctant to share them and their ancestry with the rest of the world. He pulled the buggy into the yard and motioned to the young boy to make his way into the house, patting him fondly on the shoulder. He watched him walk up the steps and into the house, closing the door.

Looking back over the fields, he could see the lights from the house they had just left, shining through the trees. He sighed, knowing how long they had lived on this wonderful land. Almost one hundred years, he thought to himself. Handed down from his great grandfather, Trinidad Ramon Cordero to his grandfather, Travarres Arman Cordero and then to his father, Antone Mercado Cordero. He, in turn had been given a ten acre parcel in which to raise a family. Along with the land, his father had given him ownership of the families's herds, upon his marriage to his beautiful wife. At that time, his estate had consisted of five of the pure bred stallions from one of a relatives's estates in Italy and a few others from their own stock. Since then, they had acquired twenty head of the best of European stock. Smiling, he remembered the trip abroad that his father, Antone and Uncle Arman had made, finding not only the some of the last of these rare breeds, now standing quietly in their stalls, but the secret itself to their uniqueness. Pleased, he turned the team of horses into the barn, where he took off their bridles, hanging them on the barn wall. Blowing out the lantern, he walked briskly to the house, stomping his feet on the front porch to shake the off the dust. His wife looked up at him as he walked into the parlor, giving her a smile. "You have been waiting up for me, I see," He said. She smiled and stood, greeting him gently. They walked together up the wooden stairs and closed the door to their room.

CHAPTER 2

Thoughtfully, Arman looked over the cartography agreement he had been given to produce an accurate rendering of the land between the northwest coasts and the mountains of the pacific northwest. Estimating quietly in his mind, how many days a trip into the southwest mountains would take once he arrived, he walked over to the wall full of books and found the old leather journal of his grandfather. Taking it from the cupboard, he settled comfortably into his chair by the fireplace. Opening the journal once more, he started to read. How I love a mystery, he thought to himself.

It was said, that his father, Travarres, was a great visionary. This, by the people he had come to know who traveled the great trade routes though out the West Indies and China. Since the early sixteen hundred's, he and his father before him had explored throughout the country side, purchasing fine horses, cattle and other goods to sell.

Many had watched for his great team of horses and carriage as it had made it's way through their small towns. In just a few years time, the adventurer, Travarres had made a small fortune from gathering the best of purebred horses from Spain, Portugal and France. On one such trip, Travarres had come across a small grouping of antiquities which had once belonged to a great king. Arriving home with these treasures to add to their already large collection, he had made note of it in his journals. People had come from all over for glimpses of the past, which he had displayed proudly among the halls of his fine home.

Since then, he and his family had invested in unique and quality items found only in some of the country's oldest estates. This and raising horses, the purebred Andalusia breed. This trip, he thought, was the one, the one that had started the legend. Now, almost twenty five hundred years old.

Reading quietly, Arman was drawn into the beautiful landscapes and vistas of over one thousand years ago. He mused over the drawings so carefully drawn in the side notes. It looked like to him, that from much of their travels, they had acquired several large shipments from the great and holy land of Israel, as well as other parts of Europe. He read on, content that, along with the writings,

8

these same items were also neatly stored in the rooms up the stairs. An hour went by, and then another until he was done. Satisfied, he went to pack for his long journey, thinking quietly about what he had read. Just the month before, he and his brother Antone had made the trip to the land, they both loved, near the ancient city of Jerusalem.

It had been a very warm and dry day, when they had arrived, just ten miles down the road from the city. Squinting into the afternoon sun, Arman had urged the horses forward faster, anxious to meet up with the Curator of the estate. The low foothills, which were covered in gray and white rock, made stark contrasts between the green of the cedar trees.

The smell of salt, strong in the warm air was soft on the eyes, as the sun gave the walls a soft golden yellow, hinting of the past and its people. As they rode into the ancient city, Antone peered over his glasses, reading the folded note he'd handwritten for directions. The Curator's letter had indicated a detailed list of estate items for sale and a mysterious note from an old acquaintance, who mentioned that he had seen the Cordero insignia on several of the boxes. Excited by the possibility of items originally owned by his father or grandfather, he'd quickly made arrangements for travel. The estate, one of the oldest in the Jerusalem, had promised that the trip would be well worth it. They pulled up next to a large, stone building and got out, glancing at each other, suddenly nervous. Adjusting his hat, Arman strode to the door to knock, waiting silently.

A few moments went by and the door opened slowly. A tall, thin man in uniform answered, ushering him in with a wave of his hand. Antone called back over his shoulder, "I won't be long." He said. "Did you want to join me, Arman?" He laughed, seeing how his brother was already turning the buggy to the road, anxious to go see the fine horses he'd been told about on the outskirts of the city. Arman waved, calling out he'd be back to pick him up in about three hours.

"Ah... of course," Antone sighed. Walking into the building, he could see dim light reflecting off the creamy walls, that lit up the dust trails following the sunbeams. He sniffed deeply, enjoying the musty smell of old books and fabric. The guard stopped just short of the room, announcing the arrival of the curator, who walked in briskly, nodding to him. He escorted him to one of the back rooms, nodding graciously, as he closed the door. Antone sat with a book perched precariously on his knees and began to draw sketches of some of the items in the room. Walking up to the opened boxes, he took his eyeglasses out of his pocket, cleaning them on his shirt.

He put them on, sighing, taking his leather journal out of his pocket. Carefully taking notes on the sculptures, art and other objects recovered, he noted the time. He was quite surprised at the wide variety of objects and carefully looked them over, deciding which would be the best to purchase.

I must hurry, he thought, just one more box. At last, he was done. He closed the last box and tucked the notes into his pocket. He glanced at the items, happy with the list of papers, books and paintings. Intrigued, he looked over to the paintings leaning against the wall. A wooden crate lay on it's side by them, half opened. Curious, he nudged open the lid and peered inside. Inside, he saw a set of expertly crafted leather books and some loose paperwork. He carefully put them aside and found a small box made of tin, inscribed on the top with an ancient, arabic language. He shook it gently, wondering what was inside. As he did, he glanced at the door, listening for his brother, as he opened it. Inside, he found two small wrapped bundles in the softest of leather. Untying the larger one, he looked inside of it. Gasping, he stared at the heavy object, all at once, realizing how important a discovery it was. He quickly wrapped it up once more and laid it aside. Looking over his shoulder, he picked up the smaller object, untying the string and gently opening the package. It contained a smaller object, which looked like it may connect to the first, expertly crafted in the finest of manner. Excited at the discovery, he tied the package up again and put it back into the box, setting them both aside for purchase. Among the rest, were those that contained clothing and assorted fabrics. All manner of beautiful silks and brocades, had been carefully tucked away wrapped in thin, white paper. Gathering up his notes from the desk, along with some of the old leather books, he put them with the rolled drawings and paintings stacked along the wall, waiting for permission to purchase them. The guard, stepped into the open doorway, asking if he was in need of anything more.

Antone shook his head no, politely and dusting off his hands, suggested he was ready to leave. "Thank you, sir, I'll go retrieve the bill of sale for you," said the guard. "And will you have need of a cart, Sir?" He asked. Antone glanced at all the cartons and nodded yes.

Just then, a shout from the doorway below announced that his brother had arrived. He looked up as Antone came out of the office, a smile on his face, gesturing to the boxes that were being stacked by the door. They watched as the carefully chosen items, box after box were loaded onto the cart that the guard had secured for them. Antone nodded as they left the building, giving his brother a secretive look. They drove off silently, the loaded cart tied to the back bumping along behind them. They nodded to the shepherds as they passed, their dark eyes watching them carefully. A couple of men on horseback passed by, stepping off to the side and they nodded in polite salute to the Cordero's with their outfitted buggy, clearly giving them a class distinction. Antone waved his hand in a silent acknowledgment.

Asking how the afternoon had went; Antone was told that Arman had made the purchase of two mares and three stallions for delivery to their estate within the month. He laughed, "Is that all?" He asked. They bid farewell to the city, now dim, lights glowing in the early evening. A quiet peacefulness took over the land as they rode silently. The lodging just up ahead had promised a good meal and they were tired and hungry. A man waiting to greet them took the reins off his hands leading the buggy and the cart to the back where the horses were given water and oats.

Antone sank into a bed of fresh linens, after a full meal of lamb stew and bread, happy with the trip. Arman, after checking on the horses, turned in for the night. A hot and muggy night went by without a single sound. Arman, woke early, feeling the quiet comfort of the old adobe style inn. Bright sunlight was beginning to pour into the room as the smell of breakfast cooking wafted up from below.

Weary still, Antone answered the door upon hearing the soft knock.
He looked at the young woman standing in the door of his room, with a smile. "I say there, maid?" He asked.

"Could you bring me something to eat this fine morning?" She smiled back at him as she handed him some fresh towels and nodded, passing Arman who had gallantly made way for her to pass through the narrow hallway. "And a good morning to you," He nodded, pulling off his hat. Ushering him in, Antone motioned for him to sit down and have some breakfast with him. "The maid will be by with something to eat shortly and we can be on our way," He said. "It was late when we arrived and I didn't get the opportunity to show you one of the treasures I had found," He paused. "I am most anxious to tell you about it," He said. "Sit, sit, and let's eat." He gestured impatiently. He looked towards the table by the window. "If we hurry, we can be back home within one day's time," He said. "You'll be pleased to know that the travel arrangements are made with the extra storage you requested, "said Arman as he sat down at the table. "Here's to a successful trip."

The maid then arrived with their tray of steaming food, leaving it on the small table. Antone looked at the open trunk with clothes and belongings that lay scattered across the small room and the dusty boots that had been left by the bedside. "I can be ready in one half hour." They sat eating, watching the passersby below, making plans to be on their way. Another knock at the door, and Antone replied loudly, "Yes, what is it?" He paused. "Sir, we have your buggy and cart ready for you, as you requested," said the servant. He nodded at them as he stood in the doorway. "We will be on our way in a few moments, thank you." He handed him a bill folded neatly and watched him walk down the hall. Nodding to Arman, he grabbed his hat and bag and together they walked downstairs and out of the building to go home.

A month later, with sunlight streaming through the window, Antone wondered where Arman was at that very moment. It had been two weeks since he had left on the voyage which would take him, along with the parcels carefully chosen and one dozen of their finest purebreds to the America's. "Come with me, Antone, it's too great an adventure without you", he had laughed. "And who will run the place?", he had scoffed, "The women?" Nodding, "Let's go see to the horses, I think we could arrange a sale or two to finance this trip, if you insist," He said. They had walked outside and down the pathway to the large fenced in paddock, where one of the trainers was walking a one year old purebred.

Expertly putting the horse through his paces, the trainer was ordered to bring out the master's horses for a ride. Both men, quickly changed their jackets and donned their hats, walked the length of the road towards the open door of the large barn, where the horses waited, saddled. "Nice day for a ride, isn't it?" laughed Arman, patting his horse on the neck as he mounted it. Kicking its side, he suddenly took off at a full run. Antone, growled as he urged his horse to catch up with his brother. "Aaayaiii," He yelled as he took a ditch in one leap. At the end of the property, they had stopped, looking back over the land the family had lived on for the last one hundred years. Arman sighed, happy and now unsure of his course he'd set before him, not wanting to leave such a beautiful place.

And that very morning, the rocky hills above the western coast had been covered in morning mist, as Arman, had ridden hard and fast, chased by three men on horseback. Desperados, he had thought, sent by the Conquistador Jorge Renaldo. a dangerous man with a charming smile, who had wanted his horses upon arrival and more as he soon found out. Yes, he thought as he looked, they are still behind him. No doubt to rob him of the rest of his goods. Looking back over his shoulder, he saw the men right on his tail as he dodged down a steep hillside onto the desert floor, racing at a full gallop, dust flying behind him. Gasping, out of breath as his horse was, he stopped, to watch over the high desert. Still wary, not seeing any sign of the men, he continued on to the hidden mine he'd heard about from some of the seamen he had sailed with. Arman, after arriving at the western port with a stash of treasures and books, had looked to the small herd of carefully tended, horses, calling out to the dock workers to secure a paddock for him. Just off to the side, a wealthy gentleman, with a somewhat disreputable past had been watching him as the dockworkers unloaded the cargo from the ships anchored. The man lifted his quirt, tapping a young man on the shoulder as he walked past.

"You there, bring me the cargo list from the last ship that docked," He called out. "Fast, fast, go man," He said with a disdainful tone. The young man looked up as he was handed a few coins to go do as he was bid. The Conquistador, who had just finished up his business, was on his way to his carriage, when he had spied the uncertain first steps of a lovely mare, being brought down the planks of wood from the side of the large, sailing ship. Another followed, and his interest peaked, wondering who would have brought these horses by sea. An intriguing thought, he said to himself.

And then, suddenly, the stallions, one right after another appeared. His buggy stopped with a jolt. Listening, he could hear a colorful mixture of Spanish and English coming from a man watching the unloading intently. "Careful with her, she's with foal", he urged "Careful, careful with that fine lady", growling. Noting the crowd gathering to watch the horses, he waved to the dockworker, who hurries to his side. Murmurs ran through the crowd, as one after another, people pushed their way to speak with him about the horses and a possible purchase. "Go, fetch that man, at once", he spoke quietly. "Bring me all he has", said the Conquistador, pulling at his mustache. "And find out where he was going? Hurry, man, go", he shouted. The man ran to do his bidding, pushing a handwritten note into Arman's hand, urging him to look over to the side of the dock yards, where he could see several carriages in the process of picking up passengers along with shipments. Watching where the man had pointed, he noticed the fine carriage where a man sat watching him. Renaldo waved, lifting his hand to indicate to follow him. "Senior, Senior, please come quickly, my master has use of your horses and would like to speak to you about a purchase", he paused.

"Come with me and he will put you up for the night and give you an evening meal.", he said. Arman nodded politely, eyeing him suspiciously. Arman nodded politely, eyeing him somewhat suspiciously."

"Yes, I see that he has a fine carriage, but I need to unload the horses and get them to a place for rest and feed quickly, I'm afraid the way has not been that easy.", he said. "Could you send a carriage for me later?", he asked. The man quickly looked back over his shoulder and got a nod of approval from the man in the fine carriage.

"Yes, yes", he said. "Someone will be back to get you at seven this evening", he called out to Arman who stood taking off his gloves. He nodded, accepting the invitation. Two hours later, found him ensconced inside the carriage on his way to the Conquistador's hacienda that sat on top the low hillside above the sea port. Stepping out of the carriage, he stood silent for a moment admiring the beautifully kept grounds. A deep voice startled him and he turned quickly. "Come, come, Sir:, I am glad you could join me this evening", said the Conquistador, standing there in his tall leather boots and riding jacket.

"Come inside and we'll have something to eat and drink", he motioned for him to go through the open door." I am curious about your cargo you have brought with you:, he paused. "Where did you sail from, you said?" He asked. "Europe?"

Arman stood with his hat in his hands, sweaty from tending the horse herd. Looking around the elegant room, he asked, "Huh?, Oh, yes." He said. Ah, may I go wash up, first?";ooking at his dusty clothes." Quickly adding, I'd like to show you one or two of the parcels I have brought with me." He said. " Perhaps, after dinner?". The conquistador nodded and said, "Of course, sir." Calling out to the maid, he ordered her to take the gentlemen's bag to guest room and fresh towels and hot water for him. As he looked the tired man over, he quickly suggested in Spanish to the kitchen help, who jumped at his loud voice ordering a light afternoon tea be taken to his room, as well. Satisfied, he looked at Arman and smiled. "We will have our evening meal at seven o'clock," He paused. "I'm sure my staff will provide all you need." Turning to the door, he opened it to the garden patio and showed him the path to his room.

Arman walked slowly to the room provided, admiring the beautiful patio gaily decorated with painted benches and large floral plants. A soft voice interrupted his thoughts and he turned to see a young woman standing behind him. His breath caught as he looked into the softest brown eyes he'd ever seen. Beautiful, long black hair curled around her shoulders and she had a sweet expression on her face. "Excuse me?", He stuttered.

She laughed gently. "Sir, come this way and I'll show you to your room." She wished past in a long cream dress, trailing colorful ribbons of pink and purple behind her. He was mesmerized, laughing at himself. He followed her to the open door, where she nodded to the fresh linens on the washstand a tray of hot tea waiting for him. "Is there anything else you need?" She asked. "He shook his head, no. Taking his bag and giving her a kind smile, he said." No, thank you." He watched her walk down the garden path, shaking his head. Thinking to himself, how his luck had made a turn for the better, he took out his fresh clothing and laid it on the bed. Sitting, he pulled off his tall black boots, he put them aside and went to wash up. An hour later, he shook himself awake, after drifting off to sleep the comfortable bed. Going to the window, he parted the curtains and looked outside. The late afternoon sun had turned to sunset and he realized it must be close to dinner time. He quickly washed his face and hands, combing his thick mane of hair. Putting on a clean white shirt, he donned his jacket and walked out the door. Fragrant aromas of baking breads and spicy meats, filled the air as he remained standing waiting for the conquistador to enter the room. Hearing footsteps, he turned and saw the lovely young lady he'd met earlier. He smiled a polite greeting to her as she walked forward giving him her hand. He took it gently, lifting it to his lips and asked. "And what was your name, miss?"

She curtsied slightly and said. "It's Mariata, sir. And you are, Arman Ortero Cordero from Portugal, my uncle said. He nodded. "Yes, I am.: He said." Your uncle is the conquistador?" He asked, lifting his eyebrows. She laughed and said, "Yes, he is. Conquistador Jorge Renaldo. This land has been in our family for over a hundred years My uncle built this house when he was very young." "Isn't it lovely?" She asked looking around the room. "He will join us shortly." Pointing to the veranda, she asked him if he'd like to step out onto it for a moment. He nodded and waved his hand. Glancing at each other, slyly, he asked if she was just visiting. "No, sir, I have lived here with my uncle for the last year after going abroad for a year to study. "Uh-hem," he said clearing his throat. "I am leaving the day after next upon concluding business with your uncle." "My horses go to auction in the morning." "Would you like to attend?" He looked over to her. She nodded, turning to see he uncle walk into the dining room. He stopped and motioned tor them to come and join him. Arman strode forward grasping his hand and shaking it. "Thank you for letting me stay, sir." He paused. "It is kind of you." Renaldo looked at him and smiled, motioning for them to be seated at the table. Arman pulled a chair out for Mariata and then took the seat next to her.

Late into the evening, still found them seated on the veranda talking about the trades, horses and the port. The conquistador's own fine stock of cattle had been acquired by the gentlemen, who had hired him for the cartography assignment. They talked briefly about the purchases Renaldo planned to make of the herd and then bid each other a good evening. He nodded to the young lady and wished her a good night. Within a few minutes, he had drifted off to a deep sleep. Dreaming, he sees himself crossing a hot and arid desert, waves of heat radiating from the ground. Ahead, he sees a shimmering wave of air, rippling over the sand. The mountains in the distance, covered in golden light from the sunset hide the treasure, he thinks. He knows from the description he'd been given, that the mountains are in the southern Arizona territories, a new land to explore. The man, who had hired him for the exploration would meet up with him tomorrow and then onto the Rockies where he'd meet up with once more to begin their exploration of the lands. Fitfully, he tossed and turned, waking only once to see the moonlight shining through the windows.

Knock... knock... knock... Arman heard a woman's soft voice calling. He sighed, wondering what it would be like to have that soft voice calling out to him every day. Getting up, he opens the door to see the lovely dark haired young lady he'd met the evening before. "Mariata, how nice to see you this morning." He said, motioning her into the room. "It is early, sir, but breakfast will be served in the dining room." She said, her eyes averted. "My uncle has the buggy ready and will attend you this morning." She walked to the window and pulled the curtains open to let the bright, morning sunlight stream in. She turned, catching him admiring her. Their eyes met. He laughed gently. A knock at the door surprised them, both. She called out as did he, at the same time, they laughed again. A soft voice in Spanish announces breakfast is ready.

Watching him with her dark eyes, Mariata quickly bowed out, promising to accompany he and the conquistador to the auction. He washes up, dressing in the fine jacket he often wore in his performances back home. Joining them in the dining room, they ate quietly, enjoying the fruit and hot meal. Grateful for a few minutes of rest, knowing what along trip he still had before him, Arman promised to her quietly, that he'd like to return one day and see her again. She blushed, nodding. Renaldo watched them carefully, looking him over. He stood, announcing they should be on their way. "I'm glad you had a good night's sleep." He paused. "We have your horse ready, sir." He motioned to him. "After you?"

Mariata, dressed in an elegant flowered dress and cape, appeared briefly at the door, nodding at him, that she was ready. He offered her his arm, helping her into the buggy. Her uncle, stepped into the buggy and with a flourish took the reins and was halfway down the lane, when Arman caught up to them on the borrowed horse. a crowd was gathering near the stalls, eyeing the cattle and horses brought to auction, as they drove into the stock yard. "I have several purchases in mind to add to my fine stock." Renaldo said. "I will speak with you later." to Arman. He excused himself, bowing to the young lady. Finding his herd well rested, he paid the stableman for his care and had them brought forward to be shown. The auctioneer's loud voice had already started the bidding process, when a stableman motioned for him to bring his horses out. Arman, taking the reins of three of his best stallions, quietly walked the into the large corral, which was lined with dozens of local people. Leaping onto one, he kicked the horse into a high stepping trot as he led the others around the ring. The crowd clapped loudly, excited by the beauty of the horses. Two were sold off immediately. The rest were ushered in and he quickly herded them into a tight group, leading them around to be seen. Bids were quickly made and the auctioneer made known the sales were about final. Suddenly, the conquistador stood. He waved the card in his hand and motioned. The crowd went silent. One of the stablemen stepped forward to Arman, who leaned down to hear the request. He nodded, smiling. Waiting while the horses were led out of the corral and then walking to the center, he stopped. A murmur of excitement went through the crowd, as he held up his hand for silence. Laying his hands on his legs, the horse lifted it's front leg high, holding it, still. The crowd cheered. He nudged it with his knee and it took off running elegant circles around the ring, with Arman seated, head held high. They stop, and in one long elegant bow, the horse lower it's head. Amid calls from the crowd, he dismounts, bowing to the crowd and smiling to Mariata.

One, two, three herds of cattle are purchased quickly and finally a pair of well matched quarter horses, beautiful roans is brought out. Taking her by the arm, the conquistador arranges for the sale of the horses and cattle he had purchased. Nodding to Arman, he announces to several of the men nearby that they are invited to dinner that evening. with their spouses. Tapping his vest pocket, Arman, nods to them and leaves to conclude business with the stableman. Later that afternoon, preparing the tables with fresh flowers, Mariata spied him riding up the long road to the house. She waved to him as she continued to walk about the garden, cutting flowers and tucking them into her basket.

She instructs two men to carry a large, copper tub to his room and bring hot water. Dressed in clean clothes, he walked down the pathway to the main entrance, in time to meet up with some of the businessmen from town and their spouses. Music was softly playing as they gathered in the entrance.

Tap, tap, tap, tap. The conquistador had gotten everyone's attention by tapping his cane on the hard tiled floor. They went silent, waiting for him to speak. The conquistador cleared his throat and asked for their attention. "Ladies and Gentlemen, we are pleased to have you here this evening." He said. "Dinner will be served in a few moments." "Let me introduce to you some of our guests." "Upon arrival of the last ship, we met up with the Governor and his wife." Nodding to them. "And this is Mr. Cordero, from Portugal, who is here on business." Glancing over to him. "Let's be seated, shall we?" He nodded to Mariata, offering her his arm and helping with her chair. Nodding to Arman to be seated next to her. Clapping his hands, the maids began bringing out hot steaming dishes of food and drink. Conversation was lively, discussing the local port and all the latest shipments of goods from abroad. Talk turned to the horse and cattle that had been purchased and Arman was surprised to learn that the conquistador had out bid everyone and bought his entire herd, except for his own stallion. An event was talked about and lightly planned for the next spring if he was in the area to come and perform and help train the valuable horses, so known for their arched necks, coloring, strong legs and broad chests. He quietly explained that the breed was from old stock, bred originally from the mares and stallions of one of Europe's best. Several men asked if he planned to bring others over He politely said no, this trip was for exploration of the southwest mountains and high deserts. Slyly, Renaldo asked. "Pray, tell us." "Where did you come by such valuable good such as those you have brought with you?"

"Well, Sir,. as I told you, a family tradition of the Cordero's was to keep accurate renderings of the lands we had explored." He paused. "And one day, it occurred to my brother, Antone and I, just how much more land there was, across the water of course.

He laughed. "I am most fortunate to bring just a few belongings with me this trip, a few family heirlooms, you might say", he paused. "If you'll excuse me for one moment, I'll bring something out for you to see", he said. "Yes, yes, of course", said Renaldo, watching him walk out of the room.

Few moments later, and he had returned and had the small group gathered around him, excitedly examining the small box he had brought out. "This, when put to good use is the latest in cartography tools", he said. "And put to good use, it will be." He had passed the small box around, letting the men lift the instrument up and look through it, admiring the fine precision workings of it. The men were impressed by the plans he had made and wished him well.

A look passed between Renaldo and two of the men as they asked about the mines, gold and silver both that had been brought up. Some of the talk generated by Renaldo who spoke of the mines, that had been part of his own conquests before. Nodding a farewell, the men stepped out of the room and left. Renaldo watching them leave. Something about the exchange alerted Arman, who looked questioningly around. Noting the lateness, he once again gave a polite nod and shook the hands of those near him, explaining his early departure in the morning.

Dinner concluded, they mingled outside on the balustrade while music played. A few couples danced until the evening was over. Taking Mariata's hand, he guided her to the walkway, bidding the visitors a good evening. Waking up early, he readies his horse and cart, loading them with fresh supplies, along with his belongings safely stashed away. He calls out to the maid, to bring the young lady outside. She ran to the door, wrapping her shawl around her. She stopped and smiled at him. He goes to her side, clasping her hands to his, placing a small box in them. She looked inside it, tears in her eyes. She gasped at the large blue stone nestled within the white velvet "To remember me by", said Arman. "It is quite special, a family heirloom", He sighed, "I want you to keep it until I return in the spring to pick up the goods sent by my brother Antone, as he has promised." She looked at him with a tenderness that gave way to tears. "Until then", he sighed happily, holding her close.

He walked to the horse packed with his saddle bags and roll, turning to look at her once more. She waved, clutching the box to her chest, smiling at him.

CHAPTER 3

Mid afternoon, two nights into one of the hardest rides east, Arman knew that the mountain peaks he could see up ahead, was where he had planned to hide his belongings. Glancing up, he saw a river of rocks, flowing down the side of a big, yellow mountain and even from a distance, one could almost see the gold flecks shining in the sun. A soft evening light of rose and gold had descended over the mountains and low foothills. Hiding behind it is a hidden valley, full of green pastures and fertile lands, he had heard. He had heard horses behind him, several hours before and he'd paused watching. Something telling him he may have been in danger. Sighing, he brushed back his hat, looking at the area where the Spaniards had lived for hundreds of years. Finally, seeing several small homes, he made his way into the village. The wagon with an extra horse had been bought at th e port and carried the three crates and other belongings he had brought with him. Getting out of the wagon, stretching his tired muscles, he walked to the door of a small, white stucco building. The first on he outskirts of the village set into the foothills. Hearing a bellow form inside and great guffaw of laughter, he was encouraged that the visit would be friendly. A robust man with dark, twinkling eyes met him at the door. His brown robe, indicating his title as the Padre, the Father of the small Parrish. His wife, small and sweet crept up to his side, eyes wide. Surprised that their small village had been found so easily by a stranger, the immediately relaxed when Arman told them who had passed along the whereabouts of the famous but hidden silver mine to which he was determined to go to. "Hola, muchaho, esta bien?" He called out, extending his hand to him. Arman took his hand, shaking it, nodding to him. "I am Armando Ortero Cordero de Portugal, Padre", he paused, smiling. "Is this the home of Padre Olivare?" He asked. The father looked at him quietly, and nodded, ushering him inside. Calling out to his wife, he asked her to bring a cold drink of water for the tired man.

A hearty dinner with several people mingling about him later, assured him he had found a safe place to retreat to if ever necessary. After explaining by which way he had come, he mentioned the sale of the horse herd to the Conquistador Renaldo. All smiles faded. The men quickly looked at each other. One stood up, holding up his hand to get his attention. "Senior, did you say Renaldo?" He asked. "Yes, I did, Jorge Renaldo", he paused. "Why?" He looked at the men. "Is there something the matter?' They nodded, all at once, talking. He gathered quite quickly that Renaldo had been after many. Not just for their properties, but livestock and whatever valuables they had, as well. A look of alarm on his face, Arman wondered if the lovely Mariata was safe. His horse alone, was such a fine one that they had all come outside to look at it as he'd rode into the village. Now, they concluded, that this stranger, soon to be a friend, may have escaped danger. Still, taking the advice of the Padre, he was warned not to go into the mountains alone. Men played guitar, a few sang and the evening was soon over. Arman, was shown a place to sleep and gladly gave a few coins to the Padre, before turning in. Morning found him gathering his gear and making his horse and wagon ready.

The nearest mine only a few miles away, he was anxious to be on his way. Taking the neatly wrapped bundle, the Padre's wife handed him, he nodded and turned the heavily laden horse towards the mountains. The Padre calling out to him, to fire off a couple of shots if he was in trouble. He gave them a wave farewell.

The noon sun was hot and arid, as he spied the entrance to the mine hidden by cedar trees, set low on the foothills. He kicked his horse to go faster, as he climbed the narrow trail. "Ha!", he stopped. "Here it is, uh-hum, come on, let's go", He said. Clicking the reins against the horse once more, he rode to the entrance, getting off his horse and tying it to a nearby tree. The silver mine had been found by the locals many years ago and was whispered about and never discussed. It was said, it was inhabited by a great guardian of the southwest, who only let those who were pure in heart enter and then, only to take what they truly needed and nothing more. Certain death would befall any man who sought to ransack the treasures that the mine held; gold and silver, rubies, diamonds and even a beautiful stones that had been talked of.

Into the afternoon, Arman kept careful watch. Hiding some of the family heirlooms he'd brought with him, deep inside the silent mine. Sitting out under the stars, he felt at peace with this new world. Excited at the possibility of finding a piece of property of his own.

The fire had died down to glowing embers, as he fell asleep under a clear sky filled with stars. The La Azure Montano Mine, held more than gold and silver and shortly Arman was to find out what that was. The horse neighed, loudly hearing something. He awoke with a start. He jumped to his feet, grabbing his rifle, looking out over the foothills. Seeing nothing, he walked to his horse, patting it gently on the neck. Suddenly, a deep voice behind him called out. "Eh, muchacho... who are you to be here on this land?" He looked up to see two men standing there, one holding a rifle in his hand. The older man nudged his son to grab the horse and gun from him and bring it to his side, holding the gun steady, but low. "We do not want any trouble, senior", He said. "How did you find this place?" He looked him over slowly. "It is unmarked as you can see." The younger man, had carefully taken his rifle from him and was holding the reins of his horse, as they stood judging his appearance.

He started, suddenly afraid. Running his hands quickly through his hair and holding up his arms, he said. "I am Armando Cordero and I was guided here by the Padre in the village below", he paused. "I did not mean any harm to anyone", he sighed." I did as I was told in regards to the mine and have left a payment for it's use." I had hoped to find a few nuggets here and there to aid in my travels." The men looked at the small campfire and laughed, slowly and then with gusto. He smiled then, knowing they had been sent by the Padre to keep watch over him. "Mi ama Luiz and this is my son, Eduardo, senior and we have been watching you all evening", he said. "The Padre told us you had come from along ways away and were from an important family."

"We live nearby, Senior." He paused, looking at the mine. "We have watched this mountain for many years." They shook hands and the young son gave him the reins to his horse. Nodding to his son to go get their pack, he indicated they had brought some food and supplies with them. "Sir, the Padre said you may have need for some assistance and we were on our way north to see family", he looked at him. "Would you mind if we accompanied you?" Arman smiled and said gratefully, "No, that would be fine, seniors".

Smiling, he said. "Join me?" pointing to the mine entrance. The men looked at each other and nodded.

An hour later, found the men ready for food and water. They shared the bread, meat and water provided by the men and quickly made their way into the dark recesses of the mine. He nodded to the men, who quickly followed him, one carrying a lantern and one carrying a bucket. Arman felt his way back through the dark, side tunnel, motioning for the men to bring the light closer. They dug for a while, filling the bucket, making their way back outside to the creek. One more trip and back out again and they stopped to eat some of the homemade bread and meat packed by his wife, taking long, swigs of water from the canteen. Eduardo picked up a shovel and scooped some dirt into his metal pan, sloshing the water around, while Arman started to pick out a few small flecks of yellow, throwing the water over his shoulder before he went to get some more dirt from the handcart, loaded by the son, Eduardo. They continued on until late afternoon, with some success, a few silver nuggets and a few small pieces of gold flecked stone. Pleased, they stopped, loading the horse with the packs he brought with him. Lifting the canteen for a long drink, Arman sees a small rock standing out among the red brown dirt in the pail they had just collected. "Whoa!", He exclaimed. "What have we here?" He picked through the dirt, holding up the small piece of rock to the sunlight. Brushing it off, he threw it over Eduardo who caught it easily.

Chuckling, he said. "Ah, Amigo, you have found the secret of the mine!" He paused. "The color is.... Azure, blue as the sky, no?" He held up the rock, a pure light blue in color.

"Let's be on our way", he looked at the men. "It is said, once you have stone of azure, you must leave the mine." They agreed, picking up the wooden slats that covered the mine entrance and putting them back into place. Arman, took the lead, calling back to the men, as they rode. "A purebred, like this one, for you both for your accompaniment."

Pleased, they stopped, loading the horse with the packs he brought with him. Following them back down the trail, they stopped at the small home tucked away neatly behind some trees to meet up with the family of Luiz's for the evening "Armando, get up, senior," Luiz said quietly. "We will meet up with you in two days time at the village of Santa Felipe and from there we will travel with you to the north..."

He sighed and got up sleepily. Within the hour, he was on the trail riding towards the north. Following the mountain trail to the hot desert valley below, he encountered one man on horseback who eyed him with suspicion and kept on riding past. He kicked his horse to go faster, aware his plans to meet up with the businessman were just a week away.

His horses, jittery and tired, had slowed, sensing water nearby as he rode up to a narrow canyon. Dropping, suddenly into an arroyo where a small stream flowed quickly. Stopping briefly to let the horses drink, he listened, for he had heard what seemed horses behind him just a few hours before. One glance behind, telling him that Renaldo may be after more than the horses, he was after the rest of the goods. Knowing he might had sent his men out after him, he wondered if rumors of his wealth had caught up with the man.

Looking back, he thought he'd either lost sight of them or he'd outrun them. It was said, that was his style, demanding more than what had been given, as many around the dinner table had explained the evening before.

This being, the area that he had been warned about. Rustlers were known to travel through these trails. Riding quickly down the side of the small stream, he rode until he could not ride any longer. He had sent a message when he'd arrived in port, letting his brother Antone know, where he planned to be in two weeks time. The Rocky Mountains lay before him, hundreds of miles away and he sighed, knowing how long he would need to travel to get there. Packing his long, leather tube holding his maps, he had shown his family his plan for finding lost treasures, such as those from the lost Cities of Cibola, he and his brother Antone had heard about, as well as the mines talked about. Among their heirlooms, a small, mysterious painting done by Travarres, their father of mountains and seven, large trees, in fall foliage, golden yellow. Noting in his journal, these, along with some of the tales told by his parents, he loaded some of the heavy packages he'd brought with him this trip.

CHAPTER 4

Early evening, the men having met up at the foothills rimmed with pines, along the river. The men rode through forest, deep with pines as far as the eye could see. Arman had been so glad to see them both, exclaiming what a wild ride he'd had through the high desert. Desparados after him, he'd been sure. The horses picked their way along the steep, canyon trail that wound up through the trees. Along the way, they stopped to fish at one of the small lakes they came to, with Arman making notes in his journal of their path. They arrived at a small settlement of a few cabins deep with the pines. They went looking for a hot meal and fresh supplies. Arman made his bed near the campfire and immediately fell asleep. Eduardo and his father, took charge of the horses and went in search of someone who could replace one of the shoes on one of their horses, before turning in.

Deep in sleep, Arman, hears a voice speaking softly to him. He watches a valley... filled with people, followed by railroads, crossing the land He sees Diego, the oldest son of his brother, Antone, telling him the story about the land and what was to come.

Listening, he is told that his family comes to the west and settles in the high mountain valleys of the north. Then, he sees the horses and senses the danger they may be in.

Snap... crack... crack..., a loud crack of thunder wakes him up. The smell of lightning in the air. A spark of lightning and the light shone brightly across the sky, startling him.

The rain had begun to fall lightly and the thunder began echoing loudly through the canyon. A deer went running past him, he counts as many as twenty head racing by, branches cracking. Another loud snap and he jumped. A crack and a bolt of lightning hit a tall pine right in front of him. H is horse startled, jerking him sideways. He almost lost his seat. Calming his horse, he ducked under a tree and up the path and stopped, looking around. A man's voice, alerted him. He turned and saw a man standing there, just for a few seconds.

The flash of light, revealing the tall figure of a man. It was Diego, his nephew, his hat tipped low over his eyes, arms folded, staring at him, just a few yards away.

"Augh... Diego?... Diego, is that you?", he stuttered out loud. He took a step forward, his horse slipping in the wet mud. He grabbed at the reins, looking around, wondering why. Had something happened? pulling up his collar around his neck to keep the sleeting rain from getting wet. He can barely make out the dim shape of what looked like a cabin ahead. Getting off his horse, he tied it to a post near the cabin. Dripping wet, he pounded in the wooden door, calling out.

"Is there anyone here?" He pushed his weight against the door and it flew open. He looked inside the dark, musty cabin, peering into it, wondering who it may have belonged to. He looked inside the dark, musty cabin, stepping in, shaking off the wet.

Once inside, he found a small makeshift bed, table and chairs. Exhausted, he sat on a chair and tried to light his flint, lighting some small pieces of wood by the fireplace. He fell asleep quickly, warmed by a small fire in the fireplace. Tossing and turning, Arman dreamt he was high up in red rock canyons, watching cattle running, spooked. A stampede. And there in a beautiful valley, he sees seven large oak trees, the distant mountains in the background. The morning sunlight woke him as, he opened one eye and sees the small, dirty cabin. Swinging his feet over the bed, he leans down to put on his boots, picking up his pack, remembering the dream. It is then, he hears shouts from outside.

"Arman, you in there, are you here?" He hears a voice calling him. "Yes, yes, man, I'm here!", he called. He got up and opened the door to see Eduardo and his son standing there with worried looks on their faces. As they left the area, Arman tells them of his dream and guides them through the thick pines north. They come out onto a flat, and look out, seeing a wide open valley filled with pines as far as the eye can see, the mountain peaks ahead, dry compared to the lovely green below them. A rider up ahead on the trail, stops, looking back at them. He gives them a wave to come forward and look. He points down into the next ravine. Quietly, they ride up next to the man who motions that a large herd of elk are below, grabbing his rifle to make ready. They do the same and make their way down off the ridge.

A shot rings out and another. Cautious, they ride down the slope of the foothill towards the elk, who had taken off at a run. The man rides quickly, cutting out three lek away from the herd of about fifty. Amazed at the large number of animals, the men quickly adjust their plans to make time to hunt. Yelling, the man leads the elk off to the side, taking s shot. One drops. Lifting his rifle, Eduardo, who had been following close behind him takes aim and fires, twice. Another drops. The men catch up to them, yelling to each other. Arman nods, taking off after the herd. His horse expertly taking the sides of the steep ridge, he climbed up on top to have a look at where the herd had gone.

He follows it to the end of the small canyon, where he can see they crossed over into the next valley, taking a couple of final shots, downing one more. He got down off his horse and quickly went to work skinning the elk. Cutting the meat into sizes easy enough to carry, he packed all he could into his large pack, tying it on tightly. As he rode back towards the others, he could hear them laughing and talking, loading the mat onto pieces of canvas brought out from the man's pack. Carefully taking out his glasses, Luiz looked out over the valley, judging the distance to the mountain range ahead. "It looks about a day's ride, maybe two, if the trail isn't too rough going", he said.

"Yes", said Arman. "We are traveling to the San Juan River and then onto the mountains above it", he paused. "Are you from up north, sir?" He asked the man, eyeing the large pack on the back of his horse. "No, I am not:, he said." I am from the South Dakota's, Sir, born and raised." He got down from his horse and walked over to where they stood. "Followed the North Platte down into the Rocky Mountains and from there, I've been following along the red rock canyons." He said. "Trap beaver, mostly, a few bear here and there." The men nodded as they worked cutting the meat and putting it aside. "Water, nearby?" Arman asked. The man laughed. "Water?" He smiled. "Yes, there's water." He said."Up through the pines, you'll come out onto the biggest, meanest desert you've ever seen." He sighed, heavily. "I guess its the Colorado River that empties into the canyon." He looked about, getting his bearings. "For now, I'd say, let's ride down a mile or so." He said quietly. "I know from looking out over the top, that there is small lake nearby." They tied the meat onto the back of the horses and led them down the steep trail. Stopping, they could hear the sound of running water. The man yelled back to them, to follow, leading his horse with the elk tied onto the back until they see a clearing, where they found the small lake was, surrounded by pines.

"Let's make camp and have some of that meat." Eduardo called out to his father, tired from hard work. "I'll be fishing in the morning", he grinned. They laughed and said, "Yes, son." It was silent as they made camp, building a fire to cook some of the meat. The evening grew dark, as the men sat around the campfire, enjoying a hot meal.

CHAPTER 5

Arman climbs off his horse, looking out over the valley, dry and hot. The morning, which had been fruitful, had brought them a string of fish that lay beside the dying campfire from last evening. He had decided to map the area and it's unusual rock formations that they had seen on them way up the rugged trail. Waving to Luiz, he called out, that he'd return before dark. Riding down into the steep canyon from the ridge, he'd found a deer trail to follow. It led him out to the very edge of the deep pine forest, they had been camping in. Getting off his horse, they rested. Kneeling, he began drawing all the details he could see in the journal he kept in his pack. Just beyond, on the next ridge, he spotted a large rock, in the shape of an eagle perched high above the desert floor. He looked around for something to mark the way. This will work, he thought stacking the rocks to mark the spot where a person could look to see the great eagle sitting above the canyon.

Taking out a piece of lead, he drew a rough sketch of the area in his journal. Judging by the notes from the trapper, he estimated they were about a half mile directly south of the branch of the river that flowed to the west. The mountain range behind, leading the way into the northern territory past the great lake talked about Picking his way back down the hillside to where the men were gathering their belongings, he made an estimate of how much time it would take to travel to reach the lake. He called out as he approached. "Let's move on, I've found a place to explore on the way north". "It's just ahead". They stared in awe at the landscape before them, as they came up out on top of the ridge. From there, they could see the large river that wound it's way through the valley down below. From here, they could make out the rock stack, marking the way to the next canyon. Just beyond, Arman told them was the passage way north they were looking for. Eduardo led the pack horses down the hillside towards the river, with the men following behind. The afternoon sun outlined the canyon walls, making deep purple shadows between the sheer red rocks. Passing the marker, Arman called out to stop near the entrance to the canyon. Pointing out the eagle rock to the men, he asked Eduardo to climb up the ridge to see what it looked like from above.

Eduardo struggles up the narrow, rocky ravine, using his hands and feet to brace against the walls of a crack in the canyon wall. Looking back over his shoulder, he called out to the men below. "Almost there!". He stops at the top, a short distance from the eagle rock. "The river flows all the way to the end of the canyon, "he yelled to Arman.

The men motion for him to go on higher. He turns and continues to climb up the ravine until he came out onto a ridge. Out of breath, he stops and looks around. Right behind him, he can hear the men following on horseback just below on the hillside.

He pulls his binoculars out to scan the canyon below, seeing if the way was clear.

The enclosed valley was full of pines and scattered aspens. A rocky slope of gray rock tumbles out of an opening into the open meadow below. Eduardo looks through the glasses and sighs, waiting for the men to pass by underneath. The eagle rock, directly in front of him, he crawls carefully towards it. Reaching it the same time, they stopped to look up at him, he waves. It is about one hundred and fifty feet tall, orange sandstone with cream streaks. He stared at it, amazed and looked all around the valley below it, seeing about a mile away, smoke.

Cautious, he called out to the men below, "I see camp, maybe, there is smoke, about a mile to the west." Arman nodded, already on his way up, climbing through the shale and slippery rocks. Reaching him, he took the binoculars and surveyed the area. Giving a quick glance to Eduardo, he tells him to descend quietly, not sure what to expect. Taking the first trail that led along the creek, they crossed over and into the small valley, wondering who may be up ahead. Late afternoon sun had set, making the canyon cool and dim.

A bird calls, high, a tittering sound, Arman pulls his rifle slowly out of the holster and holds it, looking back at the two men. The horses step about nervously, hearing something. Another bird call and then answering call to the left of them, high on the ridge. Arman agreed and led them out through the narrow canyon opening, past the bend that hid the eagle rock. Stopping, he let the men know that he'll catch up with them and then grabbing the reins of the lead pack horse, he rode back towards the opening and waved them on. Taking heart, he felt it was the right place and there it was,. just as he'd hoped. A dry river bed, they had crossed over a while back continued on for some time, but from above, he had spotted what looked like a waterfall. Sure, that the stories were true about rustler's hiding in the canyons, he made his way quickly for fear of being watched to the end of the dry river bed. Looking down into the horseshoe shaped falls, now dry as a bone, he wondered when the last water had ran through the river. Once full, it must have been a good twelve feet across and at least, two or three feet deep. The falls were a perfect place to hide the goods, he laughed to himself. Taking the steep incline down in to the river bed, he judged it to be at least forty feet tall.

Deciding on the way back to where the men were waiting just a mile or so down the river to call the falls, Wild Sage Falls from all the beautiful purple and dusty green sage that surrounded the area. Dusting off his hands, Arman gestured to Eduardo to bring him the large parcel off the mule. "Uh-hum, that will,do", he said, tiredly. "Come, let's go quickly from the river, the way will be earlier with one of the horses freed from the heavy bundles. Dropping their packs on the ground, and tethering the horses to the trees nearby, they make camp for the night.

A bright ray of sunlight hits the wall behind them, lighting it up like a lantern. Luiz squinted, as he sat up, looking at the scene before him. He hears a low, tone that fills the air, echoing through the canyon. Must be the wind, he thinks. Nudging his son awake, they get up and stir the embers of the last evening's fire. Luiz was kneeling by the fire, stoking it with wood, when he looked up and saw a shadow on the ridge above and then it was gone. He looked again, wondering. Then he noticed, along the sheer wall of the deep red sandstone, a light reflecting, shining gold. His heart leapt. He looked over to Arman, still sleeping, gently calling to him to wake up. Opening one eye, he looked at the men, sitting there with a surprised look on their faces. Eduardo pointed to the canyon wall and laughed. Arman stared in disbelief at the large shape, shining golden. He then, laughed out loud, "This is it, most certainly", he said most quietly, nodding.

"We have found the spot". He grabbed the journal out of his pack and scribbles some notes, nodding to them to get their gear ready to leave. "Come, men, we've got a long ways to go", he called out to them, as he turned his horse towards the canyon entrance.

CHAPTER 6

Ten years has gone by, he thought as he rode up the trail to the entrance of the mine.

"Uh-hum, uh-hum", he said to himself. "Get up, now, he called to his horse, hitting it on the rump with the reins. The cart loaded with supplies had rumbled along for the last two hours and he was weary of the rocky trail. Just beyond the pines, the entrance lay hidden. He had found it quite by accident while exploring through the territory. The mine, produced both silver and gold and even on a rare occasion, a small diamond or two. With his horse, mule and cart he'd managed to clear the opening enough to work the small natural cave for the last ten years.

Stopping, Arman takes his gear and mining tools that had been scattered on the ground and goes into the mine entrance. Picking up his satchels, he took one last look at the morning sun, rubbing his horse's nose for luck, he says to himself. He walks into the dark recesses of the mine, working for half the morning. After filling his bag several times, he begins packing them out to the cart Walking down to the side creek, a tributary of the rushing river nearby, he kneels, unhooking the metal pan from his belt, dipping his hand into the dirt and rocks form the canvas bag. Sprinkling some water into the pan, he dipped the edge carefully into the water. Almost instantly rewarded, he sees flecks of gold and even some silver showing. Quickly, he picks them out and puts them into his pocket. One, a shining piece of rock, catches the light as he wipes it off on his chest He holds it up to the sun, sighing. Placing it into a small leather bag, he climbs into the cart and starts down the canyon to his cabin, a few miles down. Built by own two hands, Arman had finished it after his last trip west to the seaport, where he'd managed one more trip home to Portugal before arriving back in the land he found he loved. Smiling, Arman leaves the surveyor's office, the next day, with a few hundred dollars in his pocket. The small shining stone he'd found the day before, worth more than the small silver nuggets he'd found. He fumbled with the piece of folded paper in his pocket assuring him that the claim to the mine belonged to him. His white stallion, his most prized possession, nickered and slowly walked to his side, nudging his shoulder. He climbed into the saddle, speaking softly to him. "Uh-hum, it's a good day, uh-hum."

Twenty years later, rubbing his hand over the initials carved into the tree, Joachim stood recollecting all the stories of his Great Uncle Arman Cordero. Following in his footsteps, Joachim had made his way over to the America's along with his nephew, Jean.

They, determined, like he, that it was a great adventure awaiting them. The belongings which had already been gathered included a good many heirlooms, most of which had been purchased and collected by his grandfather and Great-Uncle years before. These lay underneath the dusty throws, as Joachim stood looking at the cluttered room.

Sighing, he had read the cargo list from three different ships, one wagon and one horse drawn cart, when the first shipment from home had arrived. Glancing at the boxes being unloaded, he thought to himself, "Ah-hah, there it is", remembering the carved wooden box that had always sat on his grandfather's desk. The shipment was left by the men who had loaded it for him after giving them half a month's wages for their services. Putting one of two heavy journals under his arm, he moved a set of old binoculars and a well used compass out of his way, carrying them to the table. Looking among the hidden folds of faded fabrics and finding some small boxes filled with some small gemstones, he also found an old coin. A definite piece of gold tucked away in an envelope intrigued him, wondering where it had come from and finally, the rolled up sketches and paintings, that had been concealed in a old, leather tube.

Joachim uncovered the oil painting, covered with a soft cloth that hid lay hidden beneath soft cloths since it had arrived.. He wondered at the beautiful painting of Spanish horses, which had been treasured by the family for many years. He stood it up on the fireplace mantle, calling out to his wife to come have a look. Planning s on sharing the items later with his nephew Jean, and the rancher, Quinn Whitaker who has contracted with them to find cattle lands to purchase. He could hear them coming, as he looked out the window, noticing the hour. His nephew Jean Leandre Cordero, a young cartographer, he and Quinn Whitaker finally arrive driving a fine set of matched quarter horses and new buggy. As they gathered that evening, they talked of finding the treasures of the Lost Cities of Cibola and other legendary treasures, as told to them by some of the locals natives. The next morning, the men leave for a two week journey.

"Hear that?", Quinn asked. Looking back at the two men hard pressed to keep with him, he laughed. He had taken off at a run after freeing one of his best horses from the team that he used to drive his buggy. First, me first, he thought as he headed for the river. A three day ride's worth of dust and dirt covering him. Clothes lay scattered over the bushes, as the men washed up. The horses and mules are fed and watered and the men settle into camp. Joachim unpacked his leather knapsack, repositioning his eyeglasses to see better. He fumbled in his pack for a thin pencil lead to make some notes.

Rolling up the strings on his binoculars, he puts them away in his bag. "It looks like about a day's ride from here, before we reach the trail, don't you think?" He asked.

Tiredly, he puts his hat back on, looking at the high mountains in the distance.

Santiago, who had been gathering up his belongings, looks around for Jean, who had went looking for fire wood. He sees him up on the hillside, his arms full of sticks and wood. He holds his hand up to avoid the glare from the setting sun, waving to him. Jean had caught sight of a formation of unusual rocks and had gone to investigate. Walking over to the rocks, he knelt, spotting something low. Symbols had been scratched into the surface of the granite, surprising him. He looked around, thinking it must be out in the middle of nowhere and yet, here were signs of life. It looked old, he thought to himself.

Later, telling Joachim, "I knew I had seen something like that before." He laughed at his startled gaze, as he told him to stop right there, going immediately to find the old journal in his pack to show them a small sketch his Uncle Arman had drawn. It was a pile of rocks and a notation about the horse symbols on it. "I knew if we came in through that draw, we'd be close to where Arman had mapped, but to find this so easily, I'm amazed." he said, shaking his head. "That means the trail is right here close by."

He shows them the small sketch of the rock formation drawn in the journal, throwing the journal over to Quinn. "Have a look and see", he said. They walked back to the camp. "This will have to hold you til we find some fresh game", Joachim said as he tossed some jerky to Jean out of his saddlebag. Jean catches it and tucks it in his vest with a nod of thanks. "I think I'll see what I can catch us for dinner," walking off towards the river with his fishing gear,

Joachim had sat down to rest his back against a fallen log, looking through half closed eyes at the scene before him. Up on the ridge, he could see Jean carefully picking his way over the top about a half a mile away, with a deer that lay across the back of his pack horse. Picking up the small string of trout, he walked back to the camp. as Jean calls out riding towards them. "Just over the ridge yonder, I think I saw...", he paused. "Come have a look." The men looked questioningly at him, as he pointed to the ridge. They followed him back up towards the rock formation and stood, looking out over the valley below. They could see the mountain range in the distance and a long, low valley filled with pines. It was then, Joachim spotted them, just as Quinn did. They whooped loudly to each other. There stood the stand of trees. Grabbing his binoculars from his pack, Joachim looked through them and pointed to the now, familiar landmark. Smiling at him, he hands them back to Quinn, "Here take a look."

In the middle of the high summer grass, there stood the large oak trees, in full foliage. They took. off down the slope at a run, stopping just short of the trees, out of breath. Just as drawn by Arman, planted in a row, were the trees. The mysterious trees, he had indicated were the key to the treasures, rumored about for over twenty five years. Right in the middle of the wilderness, just as his grandfather had said in the last letter to him. His brother, Arman, who had mapped the area many years before, making sure every detail, had been saved in his letters to his brother overseas. With tears in his eyes, Joachim rubbed his hand over the trunk of the first tree, turning to look at his nephew and Whitaker.

Noticing the river running nearby, they decided to camp nearby the trees the next evening.

Reading later in his journal, Joachim happens upon the notation that instructs them as to what to look for next. The symbol which had been carved into the first tree was the element for gold, AU. Pointing back the way they had come, he threw back his head and laughed and said, "We were on the right trail all along."

CHAPTER 7

Early, the next morning the men paused at the mouth of the canyon, giving it a good look over. The canyon revealing shades of deep purple and grey as they rode down through the winding walls of granite and shale. Stopping at last, at the top of a high ridge, they look out over rolling hills of green pine, fir and quaking aspen. "That's it, look there to the west," he said as he pointed below.

"Beautiful....", he sighed. There, standing out among the red rocks, spires and green pines was the eagle rock, just as drawn by Arman. It stood high above the canyon floor, about a mile away from where they stood. "Well, do we go up, Whit? ", he asked. "What do you think?" Without even answering the Englishman took off at run down the slope towards the rocks ahead. "Aaaayaah... Aaaayah!" He called out for them to hurry. Joachim hit the reins against his horse's neck and took off laughing right behind him, Jean following with the pack horses.

Whitaker reached the top of the ridge and walked his well trained horse around the rock, looking it over from the bottom, amazed at it's size. He looked back a the men below and called out to them. "I don't see anything... but what a beautiful valley" Motioning to them, he shrugged and looked out over it. Suddenly, the light catches and he sees something. A curve in the canyon wall had made him look once again. But here, a hidden canyon? He called out to the men to go forward down the narrow ravine and he'd meet them at the bottom. Meeting them, he rode forward towards the bend in the wall, telling them what he'd seen from the Eagle Rock. Looking up at the deep maroon shading on the canyon wall, they saw what looked like shields, painted shields set deep into the canyon wall. Two of them, one slightly higher than the other, indented, large as life on the canyon wall. Joachim nodded and kept riding up to the canyon wall, a grin on his face. The shields were about half way up the side of the twelve hundred foot rock wall, just as had been drawn in the journal. The men glanced nervously at each other. The horses, slightly agitated, stepped briskly around the area. Quick to react and highly trained, they seemed to sense something.

Suddenly, a whoosh of air blew past them startled them, leaving dust clouds in the cream sand.

A low, long wail, echoing, high above the canyon walls had begun. Startled, the men looked at each other in surprise at to where it came from.

"Aauuugh...cargo manchucha....", Cordero laughed out and yelled, racing forward.

"Agua...aqui, Eeeeyahhh!", yelled Jean, kicking his horse with his heels. Just around the next hill, they stop. Whitaker sees it first, a dry river bed of pure, white sand, leading to an abrupt drop from a large, horseshoe shaped waterfall, lined with red and black rock.

"Follow me", Jean yelled as he kicks his horse with his heel, dropping down off the side of the steep river bank. Whitaker sidesteps carefully down into the river bed below the falls. Joachim backed up his horse about thirty feet, kicking his heels into its side.

The horse reared up on its hind legs and took off at a full gallop, soaring over the side of the river bed, landing on the ground below the falls, sand flying. He spun the horse around laughing, looking back at the falls.

A thin drizzle of muddy water cascaded down the middle of the rock falls, indicating it had been a very dry season. Underneath, vines clung to the sides, where they could see a tunnel had been burrowed out by the natural forces of water. Looking each other, they followed Joachim to the base and got off their horses, ducking their heads to walk into the tunnel.

About five feet in, he pointed out some natural pockets that had formed in the sandstone and motioned to the men to help look inside them. Jean stopped and reached up inside one with his hand., feeling around. Turning, he looked around til he found a large rock to step on, dropping it by the hole in the wall. They watched as he poked his hand into the opening. Feeling something, he grabbed a stick and poked at it, telling them there is something big at the bottom of the hole. "It's heavy," he gasped, as he reached in and pulled out a large object wrapped in cloth. He motioned for the men to help pull the object out, where they dropped it onto the ground. Joachim climbed up and reached into the next natural indentation and pulled another cloth bag out, dropping it to the floor of the cave. Coins fell from it, as the torn and dirty bag dropped to the ground. Their eyes opened wide at the find, looking at each other.

Suddenly, Whitaker yelled, "Did you hear that?" Turning to the men,"I said, did you hear that?" They looked up at the sound. A low rumbling had begun, sounding like thunder rolling. Water, a lot of it had begun to fall down over the falls, making an incredible loud noise. They looked at each other, running, half dragging and carrying the bags to the entrance. Large sheets of muddy water fell as they ran through it, splashing through the water already starting to flow down the dry river bed.

Their skittish horses danced back and forth, as the men dragged the bags to the side of the falls. Lifting the bags onto the pack horses, they tied them on.

The sound grew louder as the water fell, and then suddenly a lull, silence ensued. They looked at each other with surprise. A rush of water poured over the top, and then another. At full force, gallons of water flowed over the top, filling up the river bed in torrents of water. Stunned, the men gave full rein to the horses, kicking up water as they took off down the river bed and up the side. The men looked back at the river bed, shaking their heads in disbelief. Joachim motioned for them to follow, getting down off his horse, a few yards from the banks. He pulled one of the heavy bags off the horse and let it drop to the ground. Together, they untied the old, cloth bags and looked inside. Pulling out a large object, they stared at it, not realizing what it was until he finished unwrapping it. Bending down he picks it up, surprised at how heavy it is. Jean sees a small wrapped package fall from the bag and picks it up. He unfolds the soft leather to look inside. He holds it out for them to see a bright gold metal piece. Heavy, it looked like it fit into a halter for a horse. Looking, he could see that several gems were set into it, along with a small rounded spot, empty as if a stone had been taken out.

Coins, scattered all over the ground as Whitaker leans over to pick up the bag. Jean began to pick them up, noting they were Spanish gold, old coins. The other bag was quickly opened up by the men, who saw it contained a second shield, in just as good of condition as the first one. Tears filled Joachim's eyes. They had found part of the family heirlooms talked about by Arman to his brother, Antone in his letters, home. Whitaker, looking up, sighed and pointed at the wind bearing down hard at them. With a heavy sigh, he suggested, "We'd better get going." The dust kicked up as the wind became fierce, making it hard to see in front of them. A sound, like a trumpet echoing high above in a low tone, echoed over their heads.

The canyon, north of the river was their destination early that morning. The men had concluded it was the best route to follow through to the northern territory and were anxious to be on their way.

Stopping for water and rest, Jean had taken off on horseback over the next hill to look for deer and elk to hunt, knowing how good a fresh piece of meat would taste to them, having been living on fish and a rabbit or two the last few days. He was halfway through the small, pine filled draw, when he stopped, thinking he had heard something. Looking over the canyon below him, he could not see anything... but there, there it was again. The sense that something was about to happen.

He rode down through a small meadow and out onto a steep, narrow trail that wound along the canyon wall. Glancing back, he judged the distance back to to where the men were and shrugged, kicking his horse to go. There it was again, a horse neighing and along with that, the sounds of people shouting. Curious, he rode quickly towards the sounds. Coming down out of the pines, he could see just below him a trail hugging the mountainside. He slowed his horse, side stepped down to the trail, listening. Just ahead, he saw the trouble. Four wagons, all filled with supplies, had been approaching slowly down the narrow, rocky trail. To Jean, it looked like a company of about thirty people or so, he judged.

He could see a wagon was in immediate danger. It had slipped off the trail, and was perched precariously on the edge of a cliff. The two wheels of the loaded wagon, still clinging to the rough trail, being held in place only by a struggling horse, while two men held it's reins.

Amid the yelling, people had gathered near the edge and were calling out to each other, trying to keep it from sliding further off the trail. Riding up to them, Jean jumped off his horse, yelling to them. He gathered from them that the driver had fallen out of the wagon, a good fifty feet, straight down. He looked out over the edge, seeing the frightened man hanging on for dear life to a large rock jutting out over the side of the steep canyon. Without even thinking, he jumped off his horse and dropped down over the side, shouting instructions to the startled people, who were surprised to see him appear out of nowhere. Calling out to the man, he could see by his bent head, he had been injured and was holding tight to the rock, in obviously pain. He crossed over the slope until he was to the side of the fallen man, speaking softly to him.

He called out to the men to send him down a rope. A settler, a man named Gage, grabbed his rope off his horse and kneeling down, he threw it down to Jean, who reached for the dangling rope it, slipping, almost falling down in to the ravine. He grabbed at it and caught it, holding it to him to him. Gage, grabbing the reins of his horse, led it out in front of the struggling horse and wagon, waiting for Jean to call out to him. Jean quickly making a loop and dropping it over the man's head and shoulders, helping him pull his arms through. Grimacing in pain, the man stuttered, "Got it... whew... Thank you. Taking the rope, Jean gives it a tug, testing his weight, calling out to them. "Pull!" He shouted. "Pull hard!"

Amid shouts of encouragement from the people above, Jean tried to lift the man as he climbed up the hillside beside him, holding tightly to his waist. Gage yelled, "Eeyah!" Hitting the horse lightly with a stick. Running along side of it, he looked back to see the man being dragged up slowly. Dirt began falling all around them, when the two men, who were both out of breath, were pulled to just under the trail about twelve feet, A loud yell, and people began screaming to get out of the way. Supplies were falling out of the wagon and tumbling around them, boxes and crates of goods falling to the rocks below, crashing open noisily. Jean looked behind them, seeing how far down the drop was and with a determined look on his face, grabbed tighter to the rope, pushing the man up with all his might, bracing his feet against the rocks.

The axle broke, with the sound of creaking wood, leaving the tongue connected to the horse, being held by a couple of the men. It started to fall, slipping down and then tumbling past them, narrowly missing them. They ducked as it went over and over, losing all its supplies, dropping to the craggy rocks below with a loud crash.

People yelled, trying to help pull the two men up off the side of the canyon wall. The horses neighing loudly, people shouting and the sound of falling rocks was deafening. Gasping, Jean yelled out. "Got him, I've got him, pull slowly now, he's been hurt!"

The captain who had been leading his small group of settlers, yelled down to Jean, "Are you all right?" He looked up and nodded. The man, moaned, looking up at him.

Are you all right? Are you all right? Where in the blazes did you come from? He yelled out. Several men pulled them up and laid the injured man on the ground. A few of the women folk gathered around him to help. A man grabbed his hand, patting on his shoulder, thanking him loudly. "But where did you come from, son?" asked the captain.

"Up, up above, mapping, hunting deer", he panted, out of breath. He pointed the way he'd come. Gasping as he fell back to the ground, trying to catch his breath.

The settler was laid down on the ground as people gathered around him, tending to his injuries. The Captain organized the move forward with the horses and wagons moving on ahead slowly down the narrow trail Jean, following behind talking with some of the men about the trails up ahead, explaining that the canyon opened up into a field where they could make camp. Late afternoon found the men gathered together around an open fire, Joachim introducing Whitaker to the group and showing them the maps, he and his nephew Jean had drafted so far in their travels.

Cavanaugh, the Captain,a tall, broad shouldered man with a thick mane of black hair and green eyes, gave a loud laugh of gusto at the antics of two children playing in the nearby stream, remarking how lucky and blessed they were to have come upon the men, who he was sure would be friends for a long time. The tired men and women mingled as they cooked an evening meal over the campfires. Interested in the cattle, horses and the possibilities of exploring the southwest mountains to live, they learned through listening to Jean and Joachim where the best places would be along the river they would come to for trapping and hunting. Cavanaugh listened quietly as the men around him searched his eyes for instructions, nodding in agreement that the rough trail they had come across on, had taken quite a toll. "Perhaps it is time to drop down into the warmer weather territories for the long winter," he said quietly, meeting the gaze of the family of the injured settler. A valued member, the man was known far and wide for his smithing skills and would be put to great use once they had settled. At that suggestion, Joachim nodded, pleased and immediately suggested a small valley they had passed to camp in, noting the abundance of fish they had caught just the day before.

As the women put the children to bed, gentle music filled the air as a couple of men played guitar and the group sang softly. Story after story unfolded as the trio of men told of their travels. Corderothen pulled his saddle bag off, dropping it beside him, as he knelt in the firelight, as he withdrew a large packet of folded paper from it. Unfolding it gently, he held it up in the firelight for the men to take a look at. They stared at the long lines of carefully drawn rivers and trails marked by the Grand-Uncle, Arman Cordero, twenty years before. Amazed at the territory and all they it encompassed, they talked long into the evening about which direction to go. Gage, an experienced trapper had already set the river showing several of the men how to find the best places for beaver. As they arrived back in camp, he looked up quickly at the group standing near the fire, wondering what they were about.

Nudging his way closer, he looked upon the map held by the men and felt a chill, something telling him that this was an important moment. Quinn Whitaker, who had introduced himself, was speaking of hiring several men once established which led the group to talk of their own experiences. "I'd like the opportunity to work for you, Mr. Whitaker", he said quietly. "I've been all over the southwest mountains myself with a native scout I made friends with and a man from the east, who went on to the western coasts". He peered at the map, asking, "From what direction did you come from?, Looking at Joachim. He laughed and said, "From the North Platte and down into the river gorge on our way to the red rocks spoke of by my Grand-Uncle". They nodded, having heard of the great red rock canyons in the southwest territories. The talk turned to the trees, the map, and the legend of the treasure and where they were headed. One of the men spoke up, telling a tale of what had happened along the way to one of their men.

It had been early afternoon, just a week before, when one of the men, Haynes had found himself trapped up to his chest in quicksand. Coming down into a dry lake bed, he had accidently stumbled onto a patch of unstable ground and before he could move from it, his horse stumbled, leaving him on the ground. Slowly, it started to cave in around him at each step until he could move no longer. Having stayed behind to hunt game, he was about a day's ride behind the settlers when it had happened. Now, alone, he was afraid and growing tired quickly. His horse had wandered off and there was no one in sight. Gasping, covered with mud and grit, he struggled to hold himself upright as the sand held him tight around the chest. He closed his eyes, praying for help, telling himself to remain quiet and calm. Breathing slowly, he tried to conserve his energy. The hot sun beating down on him, making the heat unbearable.

A snap... a twig breaking, He thought he heard his horse nearby. Looking up quickly, he was surprised to see a man on horseback standing just above on the ridge looking at him. The man seeing his eyes were open, yelled and came charging down the hill, dirt flying. Jumping off his horse, he knelt a few yards away, talking all at once in a strange mixture of Spanish and English. "Como" he said gently. "Come, senior." Holding out his hand, motioning for him to move towards him if he could. He looked up and managed a weak smile. Exhausted, he tried to move closer, but found he could not bring his feet forward, having been trapped for more than a day in the thickened, damp sands. "Hola... ahhhh!" He sighed. "Where did you come from, sir?, he gasped, wide eyed at the man. Watching, as the man ran to his horse, he grabbed his rope from it and fashioned a loop, holding it out carefully. Throwing once, but not coming close enough, he threw once more, this time coming near enough for him to stretch out his fingers to. He reached for it, grunting with exertion.

Talking to him gently, the man crouched down holding tightly to the rope, "Now, now, what do we have here?" He whispered, aware of the danger. Kneeling as close as he could get, he pushed a stick out to the man, telling him to grab onto to it. He reached out and took hold of the branch, curling his fingers around the end of the rope.

Pulling slowly, he held the rope with both hands, leaning back on his heels as the full weight of the man trapped was felt in his shoulders and arms. He glanced back at his horse standing patiently nearby. Grabbing at the reins, he pulled the horse towards him, getting back on his feet. "Hold on, I've got you", he yelled. "Hold on tight., here we go." Winding the end of the rope around the saddle horn, he motioned to the man to hold tight. He led the horse a few feet away slowly, watching the man struggle to free his feet.

"Ohhh!, He yelled, as he held on tight to the rope as it slid him over the wet, sticky mass of sand. Several more feet and the man was finally free of the mud. Gage quickly knelt by the man, bringing his head up as he dropped water from his canteen in to his opened mouth. The man coughed, blinking his eyes from the glare of the sun. Taking off his hat, Gage pulls the man up to his knees and tries to get him to stand up. Holding his arms, he lifts him carefully onto the back of his horse. Looking at the muddy hoof prints, he gathered which direction his horse had gone. "Mi ama Gage", he said as the rode down the lake bed watching for tracks. Nodding, the exhausted man sighed and held on tightly.

Wiping his face with the back of his arm, Haynes tells him what had happened. He had been bringing up the rear of a company going west when he had stopped to hunt, promising to catch up with fresh meat. Dropping down onto the dry lake bed, he had ridden just a few yards before he realized he was caught up in quicksand. "Been near three days, I was sure they would send someone back for me by now"., He paused. "I hadn't seen a soul", he stuttered. "Where was your party going?", Gage asked. "North, northwest, sir, like you with the settler's." Gage nodded and pointed to the trail that led up a small slope. "Let's go, we can catch up quickly", he said. It was after a good half day's ride, they saw the thin line of wagons disappearing into the thick pines just below the canyon ridge. Amid shouts of welcome, the settler's waved to them, as they rode up hard. Tired, sweaty and hungry, the men were given food and water as they told the party what had happened. Introducing himself, Gage explained he had been on his way west, when he had taken the route north following directions given him by the scout he had been trapping with. Camp planned to disband the next morning and the men shook hands good night as they turned in for the evening.

CHAPTER 8

Cresta La Puesta Del Sol, beautiful in the early morning sunlight, stood majestic against the sun coming up over the pines. The mountain range so named on the map by Arman as the way into the high deserts and red rock mountains. Noted on the side, were several draws, rivers an canyons leading to a great high desert indicated by the rough sketches as tall formations of cream and red sandstone. It was here, he had written his brother, Antone that they would find one of the places where he had left heirlooms. Glad to have the settler, Gage along for the ride, he made note of it in his journal, marking the places where they stopped to place traps, intending to come back by the same way in a few days.

Huff... Huff.... Huff.

A branch cracked loudly, startling the sleeping man who had dropped his roll to the ground, exhausted. He rolled slightly, grunting. Again, sounds of breaking twigs and branches. Then, a low nicker and another. He opened his eyes quickly expecting to see a rider appear. Hooves on hard ground woke the others who sleepily looked up. Jean jumped up, grabbing his rifle, crouching low while peering through the trees. He moved cautiously towards the sounds, looking back over his shoulder to his uncle, motioning to be silent. Following the trail the way they had come in, he suddenly looked up into the biggest black eyes he'd ever seen, staring back at him and throwing its head back and jerking away, frightened. Jean drew a breath before letting out a whoop that could be heard clear back to camp. He dropped to a crouch not wanting scare the horse which stomped nervously then broke into a run away from him a few yards. It stopped, blowing steam from its nose, not taking its eyes form the man walking slowly towards him. Jumping sideways, it turned and took off running through the pines.

Whitaker, having grabbed his gun had come up on the scene, wondering where the stallion had come from. Watching it as it ran up the draw, Jean motioned that he'll follow the horse as Whitaker went back after the horses at camp. He shouted to Joachim about the large grey stallion they had just seen and grabbed the reins of Jean's horse leading it back up the trail at a gallop. He heard Jean talking smooth and low to the wild eyed horse, who was cornered, backing up against a large boulder. He turned, nodding and walked slowly towards the horse holding out his hand. Startled, the horse broke into a run around the men taking off down the hillside. Jean jumped on his horse, that had been held for him by Whit and they took off after the stallion. Laughing, Joachim could hear shouts telling him they'd be back with the horse or else. He sighed, leaning back on his pack to rest. Grumbling about missing breakfast, he fumbled in his pack for the old leather journal, flipping through a couple of pages, read. Determined to make time, they had cut across the La Pueda Del Sol mountain range and down in to the valley they had stopped at. Making a few notes with the rough piece of lead, he looked up at the surroundings for landmarks. All of a sudden, he heard something. He stopped, seeing movement in the brush ahead. A hawk screamed, flying low in front of him over the trees, surprising him, the sound echoing through the canyon. He followed the hawk with his eyes for several minutes, watching it as it soars out over the pine filled valley. Tying his pack onto his horse, he watched over his shoulder for the men to return. Hearing talking, he looked back at the men who were returning down the trail. Jean took off his hat, wiping his face with his sleeve, arguing loudly with Whitaker about what looked like a herd of horses, maybe twenty or so, he guessed. Spanish mustangs, they were arguing.

The men gathered talking about the possibility of the horse capture. Nodding, they quickly gathered their belongings and turned back to the rocky trail they had just come down. Whitaker stopped to show them the tracks they had found, pointing the way up a narrow draw, lined with high walls of sandstone. Shrugging, he nodded, smiling.

He kicked his horse once took off at a run into the draw with the men following him. Coming into an opening, Jean stopped as his uncle, held up his hand. He looked wonderingly around, questioning with his eyes. They heard once more, a high pitched, loud wail of a sound like music, sweet and high echoing across the canyon. He turned to look at them, a surprised look on his face., at a loss for words. A strange silence once again enveloped the mountain.

"Jean, Whit... listen, did you hear that?" he asked quietly. "Did you?" He paused, looking over at Gage who had a calm expression on his face. He nodded,as well. "Where do you think that came from?" he said, looking around. The horse moved, jittery, neighing low, nervous. Joachim motioned to move forward slowly and they began to ride into the sheer walled canyon, watching ahead as they went. Talking in low voices, they could see signs of the horses having come through the draw. Early yet, the steep red walls were still shadowed from the sun coming up over the east side. Noting the distance they had come, Jean looked around for signs of water, guessing from the size of the canyon, it may be the one seen from above. Filled with sage and wildflowers, the narrow canyon hid a small creek which ran through it. Within a few hundred yards, they could see an entrance into a large side canyon, filled with pinion, large and fragrant.

Suddenly, a large black stallion broke through the brush ahead. They looked up surprised, taking off after it, waving to each other. The canyon, which would later be called Pintado, the Arroyo Pintado was long and narrow, filled bends and curves and they followed the stallion, who left behind big, billowing clouds of dust. Then coming to a stop, listening intently. "Listen to that, would you?,", Joachim yelled. "Let's go!" Up ahead, a deep rumbling of horse hooves could be heard along the high canyon wall. They looked up as the shadows of at least a dozen or more horses running at a full gallop across the ridge. Yelling to each other, they rode quickly up the rocky trail. A large natural rock bridge spanned across the canyon walls, tall and wide, fifty feet across and one hundred feet log, Jean would later write on his map. The thundering of the horse hooves above them was loud, indicating the herd was running quickly towards the bridge. Reaching the bridge, the horse herd runs across it and down the other side of the high canyon wall as they watched. Joachim let out a yell, as he rode up the side of the ridge to chase the horses. Racing along the high wall, Joachim could see that Gage had cornered one of the wild horses in small indentation. They stopped to help, watching as it reared up on its hind legs, neighing loudly, a beautiful black stallion.

Gage got down off his horse, walking slowly towards the horse with a lasso in his hand. The horse stood silent, watching him. He reached out with the rope as it moved away, nervous. He spoke softly, calming it. Slowly, he walked towards it. Within a couple of yards, the horse nodded its head and then bowed, backing up slightly. Gage quite suddenly, had tears in his eyes as held out his hand. The horse quietly bowed its head. Gage reached out and touched its face, gently lifting the bridle around its neck, talking to it softly. Whitaker leaned over his saddle, moved, tapping Joachim on the shoulder and pointed to the pack he always carried with him.

"The Arc de Miquel, mi amigo," he whispered "The horses, aah, cabella.,ahh", sighing.

Pointing to the large natural bridge that had formed an arch across the canyon, he swung his horse and broke into a run towards it. About fifty yards from the rock bridge, the canyon walls had fell into shadows of early evening, leaving a thin line of golden light across the top of the ridge. Joachim directed the three other men to ride towards the arch, telling them to look just beyond, where he could see the rest of the herd standing in the brush. Roping off the draw, they quickly did a head count, noticing there were several stallions altogether, counting the stallion already captured by Gage. "Must be thirty head or so, Spanish?", speaking softly. "Wild mustangs?" He paused looking at Jean. "That one there", pointing to the large black stallion, "Looks like one from a pure breed."

"Must have gotten lost from the Spanish who lived around here", Whit suggested. "They must water nearby, it looks like this is where they have been for a while."

"Haven't seen anything like these since before I left home", Jean sighed. "Let's make camp and we'll explore the canyon ridge for a way over,". He paused, looking suddenly at the deep orange canyon wall just ahead of him, seeing the perfect outline of a shield. Jean looked at the trail that had lead them north into the draw, sighing. He turned and asked if his uncle was ready to go on ahead. He nodded, moving forward towards it. They stopped, getting off their horses to walk around the area. The small canyon was filled with fragrant sage, pinion, with creamy white sand that led them into the deeply shaded narrow draw. Later, they would tell of how looking back, the shield had shone, brilliant gold as the sun hit the wall. It had just come up over the ridge when, Joachim nodded, thinking about the scene and the horse herd. How lucky they had been to see the first wild horse, with it's high arched neck belying a purebred bloodline. Gage and Whit had taken ropes and managed to tie off a small area to contain the herd for the rest of the stay. Catching the eye of his nephew, he yelled out suddenly, telling the men to look, pointing to the rock wall.

They looked up, eyes wide and surprised. There, along the high wall, just past the rock bridge was an indentation and shadow of what looked like a large piece of armor. Another sign. Riding closer to it, they could see right below it, a natural cave. A growl escaped Joachim as he said, "The Arc de Miquel." He looked at them. "We have found the treasure." Jean got off his horse, walking over to see what was inside the deep recess. Dim and dank, he managed to clear way the cobwebs as he brushed past overgrown twigs blocking the entrance. Shouting, he told them he could see a wooden plank covering something. He yelled for Whit to come and help him remove it. Together, they pulled away at a large wooden covering to find a bundle of dark canvas, covered with red dirt.

Joachim knelt down by the bundle, pulling it out of the dirt and dragging out into the sunlight. He started to cut the bag open, when Jean motioned to him to look up. They looked and saw a large white stallion standing alone on top of the high wall right across from them. It stomped, dancing around and neighing loudly. Rearing up on its legs, it took off at a gallop, leaving the men staring after it. Anxious now, Joachim pulled back the fabric to reveal the slow of deep gold metal. It was a shield, flat, heavy with what looked like beautiful etchings on it. They stood staring in awe at the find. Kneeling down by it, the men took turns running their hands over it, talking softly. Once again, wrapping it up carefully, Jean helped Joachim secure it onto the back of the pack horse and they prepared to leave the area, along with the herd of horses.

"Bien, muy bien, muchacho", he said quietly as he pointed to the camp. "Let's rest for the night." Talking late into the evening, they discussed the treasure which had been hidden away by Arman, while Jean made notes about the canyon and the herd in his own journal. He had ridden up on the ridge once more to judge the distance to the next mountain range, which would bring them to the high deserts shown on the map by Arman and gave them a report on the findings pleased.

Early in the morning, the men decided to take the herd north to leave at the ranch that Whit had purchased on his way in. Just a few cabins to it now, it would become of one of the largest ranches in the area, known for it's longhorns. Rounding them up, with Jean leading the way and Gage following behind, the men rode the herd back through the two main canyons, making good time. Another's day's ride and they would be within the grazing lands he, also had hoped to purchase. Calling it Dry Canyon Gulch, laughingly, Whit talked of the ranch and his plans to bring a reluctant wife in from the east soon as they made their way in. Hiring Gage and Jean immediately, they had planned the rendezvous at the North Platte River in one month's time to retrieve the lady and all her belongings. It was his wish to have the cabins ready for her, along with several good hands hired. The ranch, which sat in the bend of the river, was where one could see the large red mountains in the distance. Dry, it was not and the valley was as green as could be. Pleased, he'd promised to pay well for any man with experience to stay on with him, giving them a parcel of land of their own after one year of hard work.

Agreeing that the find be kept silent, the men hid the treasure at the ranch house of Quinn Whitaker. Taking the rest of the summer, Jean and Joachim mapped throughout the northwest mountains, often taking time out to trap and hunt.

CHAPTER 9

Late one summer afternoon, some of Whitaker's hired hands were to drive a small herd of about fifty cattle north to the largest city in the territory for sale. The wranglers, although, experienced enough, had left that morning, with not a cloud in the sky. As the day went on, a slight wind had kicked up. The smell of rain permeated the air, cooling it down considerably. Watching the dark clouds in the distance, the men could see a thunderstorm beginning to brew. Before long, fierce winds began to blow large clouds of dust out over the desert. Suddenly, a large crack of lightning nearby spooking the cattle. Bawling loudly, they began to run wildly. Along with Jean, was a young man, named Josiah Cavanaugh, the captain's son who had caught up with them as they brought in the herd of horses in from the southwest canyons.

Fast friends, now, he and Josiah would often be found hunting elk or deer. Jean waved to him now, telling him to hurry and bring up the rear before it started to rain harder. Marcellus, a tall, blond man, who had brought his own small family along the way west with the settler's had gone on up ahead leading the way through a narrow draw that opened up into the northern valley. One of his sons, Isaac raced with the herd down the draw, which was known as Painted Creek Canyon, leaving large clouds of dust behind them. A low crack of thunder rolled along the desert making the ground shake with it's strength. Large flashes of light filled the darkening skies Catching up with Jean, Isaac had called out to him, "There are a few stragglers left behind, I'll go after them and meet you in camp," Josiah nodded at him indicating the camp would be about a mile up the road.

Riding up to them, Marcellus pointed out the way. Just up the draw, he said and out on top. Looking up at the dark clouds, he told them to hurry, in case of flash floods. All at once, in flash of lightning, they saw Gage, on his stallion on the ridge ahead of them, silhouetted by the light behind him. He was there and then gone again. They looked at each other, wonderingly. The cattle had balked about going down the narrow draw, then suddenly began running quickly, startled by another large crack of lightning, which had hit the ground close by.

Several head of cattle stumbled as they ran down into the narrow canyon, with three of the men following closely behind them. The livestock were becoming uncontrollable, stampeding right past them, bawling loudly Marcellus, made a run for the lead, swinging his rope out in front of him to head them off. Just then, a bolt of lightning hit the ground, making the earth shake. Riding hard to head off the rush of livestock, Marcellus was knocked off his horse driven along by the jostling cattle. He stood, then fell to his knees, his leg injured. Pulling himself along, he dragged his leg behind him, as he managed to get out of the way of the charging cattle.

The ranch hands, who had gone up ahead, lost sight of him as they ran with the cattle up the narrow canyon. Alone, Marcellus stood pressed up against the dirt wall of the ravine, a good forty feet high, listening to the calls of the hands as they tried to keep the animals under control.

Exhausted, he fell back on his knees, heaving a big sigh. Looking up at the ridge before him, he grunted knowing how difficult a climb it would be. Thinking his leg may have been broken by the force of the cattle against him, he looked, wondering where his horse had ran off to. He tried to raise himself to his feet and once more walked forward, limping. The rain was still coming down in fierce sheets of hard, hitting water as he made his way to the side of the ravine. He slumped against it, feeling a surge of fear at being left behind. His horse, he knew was swept away with the cattle. Sighing, he felt a big sweep of wind, almost knocking him to the ground again. He dropped to his knees, saying a silent prayer. Taking a deep breath, he began yelling loudly above the rain, but still could not hear an answer. The hands were almost a half a mile away by then, heading north. Heaving a big sigh, he dragged himself up to the side of the ridge, shaking with the effort.

A crack... lightning.... crack.. a low rumble. Lightning filled the sky with large jagged streaks of purple and orange. Silence, all at once, Marcellus looked around him. The air had grown still. Over his shoulder, he felt the wind begin again and he turned facing into wind. His face registered shock as one of the largest wind tunnels, he'd ever seen was coming right at him, bringing with it a huge cloud of dirt and debris. He quickly looked around for cover, not knowing where to hide. Seeing along the ridge, a row of juniper trees, he dropped to his knees, crawling as fast he could towards them. Reaching them, he crouched watching as the wind tunnel made its way past him, obliterating the sky in darkness for a few minutes. Holding his hand over his mouth, to keep the dust out, he wiped his eyes and face, covered with the mud and grime. Rolling thunder rang out in the distance with the fast moving winds. It had been close, too close for comfort. Thinking how he must move out from beneath the tree, he stepped forward, walking several steps. Slipping suddenly, he felt the ground give way beneath him as he found he was too close to the edge of the ravine. Taking another painful step forward. he fell to his knees in pain.

The ground broke loose beneath him, tearing away like fabric beneath him. He grabbed wildly at the dirt and shrubs as he slipped back down into the ravine. Lightning flashed. Suddenly, he felt a hand grasp his arm. Another grabs his wrist and he found himself being pulled up and over the edge by strong arms. Looking up to see the stern face of Gage, holding him firmly against the edge, he stuttered and heaved, trying to catch his breath. Gage wrapped his arm around his waist, lifting him as he lead him over to his horse. Holding the stirrup, he helped him climb up and over it, telling him to hang on tightly. Climbing on his horse, he turned it towards the north and took off at a run across the muddy ground. The evening sky was still dark and windy, smelling of rain. Following the cattle trail, now easy to see with the muddy tracks, Gage and the exhausted man made good time, reaching the others who had gathered together. Somewhere in the herd was Marcellus's horse that had been driven along with them. They looked up surprised at Gage and he riding in. Helping him down, the men explained what had happened. Later, they gathered around the campfire, preparing a meal and resting. One of the young men hired to drive the herd, brought his horse to him and tethered it to the nearest tree. Marcellus, in charge again, quickly established the plans to move forward the following morning, sat with a stick tied along his leg to keep it straight. The others gathered wood for the fire and after tending to the horses, took their turns keeping the herd along the parameter.

As the evening sky, turned a dark grey as the stars began to come out of the clouds, he thought he heard humming. He paused in his thoughts, listening. Yes, it was, a man's low voice, softly humming a ditty, not too far off in the dim light. He looked up, curious, watching as the rickety sounds of wagon wheels against hard dirt and horse hooves came closer. In the dim light, a man appeared, pulling a small wooden wagon behind him.

He waved as he entered the campsite, nodding at Marcellus, who waved him in. "Come, join us, old timer," he said loudly. "What brings you all the way into the open desert after such a dreadful storm?" The man laughed and in a deep, raspy voice said, "Why that's nothing, son, I've seen tunnels that size and bigger all the way across the lower deserts."

Getting down off his horse, he smiled at Marcellus who looked at him like he'd never seen such a sight before. Not a hair out of place, the man was clean and dry despite the wet weather; he most surely had come through. Later, around the fires, he told tales of the western mountains. "Copper, sure, I've seen copper... egads, it comes up from the ground in droves:, he said, laughing. :Now, what they want, is silver." "Hey, I have something to show you from my last stop." He got up slowly and walked over to his wagon, fumbling around in the back. Carrying a bag back to the fire, he fished around in one and then, smiling widely, held up a large nugget, golden in color., tossing it to Marcellus who caught it easily, looking at it.

Surprised at the size of it, he remarked on the color of the obvious piece of gold. "Name's Arman, sir., that one there is a pretty good size, but look at this." He held up a large rough nugget about the size of small ball. The man's eyes grew large as he looked it over. "Is that silver?" He asked. Laughing, he nodded. "Name is Marcellus. My son, Isaac is out tending the herd and that there is Josiah, pne of Whitaker's men. Pointing out a figure in the distance, "That's Gage, a man I owe my life to."

He sighed, "Got caught in the draw when the cattle stampeded," he nodded to it. "Hurt my leg some, it maybe broken.. don't know," he wheezed, looking at him. Pointing to the wagon, Arman said, "Be glad to take you into town if needed, son... here you keep this, get that leg tended to by a good doctor", tossing him the silver nugget. He walked over to his wagon, pulling out a large wooden box, which he carried it over to the light of the fire. A couple of the men had gathered around, complaining over the jerky they had dug out for dinner the night before.

Introducing himself, the old man had quickly made himself to home, bringing out some beef he had wrapped in a piece of cheesecloth, along with some potatoes which he expertly peeled, all while the men watched, listening to his tales of the desert. Mumbling, he opened a small leather bag and sprinkled some herbs onto the cooking pan of meat. Before long, a tasty stew was enjoyed by the men who argued over the last of it, while finding places to sleep near the fire. The old miner dozed, himself, tired from his ride.

The air still and cool from the rains, not a sound, but a few of the cows lowing not far off. Horses nickering in the distance awakened them and the men looked out into the dark desert. Drawn by the light of the fire, Joachim, Jean, and Whitaker rode into the small camp, yelling out a gusty hello to the men who had been dozing by the fire, "We caught up with you, Marcellus," said Cordero. "What in the blazes happened to you?, looking at his injured leg. They began talking at once, while Whitaker quickly got the news that all the cattle had been accounted for despite the thunderstorm. Isaac, looking around said quietly, "The old man, where did he go?" He paused, looking at the men. "Did you see where he went?" He said in a low voice. "Didn't hear him leave, did you?" He asked Josiah. Maybe you passed him on the way... did you see an old man pulling a wagon?" He asked Whitaker.

Tired, rubbing his eyes, Joachim shook his head no. "No, no one, why, what's this about, Isaac?" He asked. "Must have needed to be on his way, I guess." said Josiah. Marcellus, who had gotten shakily to his feet, hobbled over to the fire. Looking down, he gasped and pointed. Spread out like a Christmas gift was a paper, weighted down by a small leather bag. Marcellus bent over and picked it up, holding it gently, knowing the old man had left them some of the gold nuggets. Peering into the bag, he laughed, his voice hoarse, "Why the old man has left us enough to pay for the trip and then some."

Whitaker had came close, watching over his shoulder. He sighed, leaning down and picking up the piece of paper, while he took off his leather gloves. Fumbling in his vest pocket, he found his eyeglasses and put them on. Unfolding it quietly, he held up to the firelight. "I think it looks like it maybe a deed or something."

He moved closer to the fire. Why, it sure is, it's to a mine!", He paused, looking at Joachim who said. "Let's have a look", holding out his hand. Taking it from him, he, squinted as he read it, smiling. Distracted, he gave it back to Whitaker who glanced at the name on the bottom of it and sighed heavily. Sitting down on the ground with a hard, they grinned at each other, then laughed and then laughing with such gusto that all the men hid their smiles for a moment before laughing along with them. With surprised looks on their faces, they gathered there was more to the deed than met the eye.

"It's the Cordero gold and silver Mine", he shouted loudly, laughing. "How can this be?", he shouted. "Arman, you said his name was Arman?" Joachim who had handed the deed to Isaac, took off into the dark trying to see where the old miner could have gone to. Calling back to them, "He's nowhere to be seen... but what is this?" He walked to a large pile of fabric on the ground near the horses tethered. Bending down to look, "Oh, my, oh my, Isaac, come help me, would you?" Together, they carried the heavy bag over to the fire and dropped it onto the ground. Kneeling down by the satchel, dust covered and old as the man had been himself, he pulled away the twine that had closed it and opened the bag. Nodding to Whitaker, Joachim poured out some of the contents onto the saddle blanket that Isaac had ran to get off his horse. "Come, see this boys, have you ever seen anything like this before?"

A pile of coins, old gold and silver lay on the blanket. They shook their heads, talking all at once. Digging into the bag, he carefully unwrapped the package in the bottom and pulled it free, breathing heavily with the effort. Lifting the heavy object out, he dropped the aged canvas aside and stood it on the ground for all to see. It was an exact duplicate of the ones already found, a large, polished silver shield, gleaming brightly in the firelight. The men let out a whoop, laughing out loud. Joachim, with tears in his eyes, tells them of the two shields they had found at the horse shoe falls and the brilliant gold one found at the Arc de Miquel, making the total now four. Grinning broadly, Joachim asked again, if the man had been real flesh and blood or not. The men nodded, indicating he had been just that, but an angel in disguise, riding on a pure white stallion.

CHAPTER 10

Hot sun beating down on him, Arman wet his lips with his flask, conserving the water. Only a few miles to go, he told himself,. Judging the mountain range off in the distance, he gathered he could make it in one day and then it was down of into the prettiest green valleys, he'd ever seen, on his way to the lovely lady that had captured his heart. He'd worked his way up and round the tallest mountain peaks, braved the coldest winter he'd ever been through. All in all, two mines had been worked, one he'd found, quite by accident, he laughed to himself. Accident, for sure, almost a sheer fifty foot drops into the falls. What a place to hide a silver mine, he thought. Having spent most the long, summer exploring around the peaks, he'd come across the falls, two large steps dropping down into a coursing river which led out into the valley floor. The valley, full of elk and deer, rich in fields and green meadows for grazing, he'd long decided it was the place he hoped to live in the rest of his life. Evenings, found him, sitting alone, by the fire, thinking about the beautiful woman he had met upon arriving in the sea port over a year ago. Glancing up, he caught sight of the tall trees just off to the side. Musing silently, about the sturdy trunks and golden beauty of the falling leaves, he thought about how to hide the rest of the treasures he had managed to procure and keep from the family heirlooms.

Now, taking his time across the high desert, he was glad he had made the extra trips down the narrow trail into town, where he had cashed in on the nuggets he had found. Two large golden nuggets had paid for his piece of property, and one more bag of silver had made the payment final for the mine, now in his name. He sighed at the long year of hard work he'd put in, establishing first, himself, as an expert cartographer and now a property owner. After, seeing off the friends, father and son who had joined him on his way north, Arman had taken the high trail up into the forested lands that connected to the North Platte River.

A series of stops had led him down the river, along with a couple of explorers from the eastern coast. One of the men had given him his first muzzle loader shotgun, which he long since treasured and the other, a man by the name of Cook, was an expert at trapping. Cook, having been sent out by an early group to locate the best way over the Rockies, had been incessantly talking about the wealth of fishing and hunting along the great Rio Grande River which ran through the southwest territories. In a hurry, to get back to it, he'd led the men on a wild ride through the red rock canyons and in their travels, had discovered a wide open and vast array of magnificent rock formations, the likes of which no white man had seen before. From that point on, Arman and the three men had traveled further south down in to the Rio Grande valley, following the great river through some of the most plentiful trapping and fishing sights they could find. A native scout, who had caught up with them along the way, told them of the trail, which would become known as the Old Spanish Trail, the best place to find trading posts, who would argue with you about the price of the furs and pelts. That, being the only way to make a living for those who lived in the mountains, trapped beaver, deer and buffalo. Luiz and his son, had stayed along the edge of the pine forest they had come up through intending to establish a trading post. Excited, by the small nuggets, Arman had given them to start the trading post, the men had made one long trip back down through the pines to the home of Luiz's family and for Arman, one day's journey to see the lovely Mariata, the niece of the Conquistador Renaldo.

A warm welcome, good food and some sleep and he was ready to ride out that next morning. Packing his gear tightly, he gave Luiz's wife a hug and kiss on the cheek, thanking her for the food packed away in his saddle bag. Shaking the man's hand, he promised to return within two weeks, bringing a load of goods from the port which they planned to sell at the trading post. Camping out under the stars that evening, he judged the distance to the western range where he could look down in to the fertile green strip of land, near the coast. Holding the packet of letters he'd received all at once, close to his chest, he held them to his nose, smiling before putting them back into his pocket. A man, who had traveled all the way through to the small village, had brought them with him and left with the family, he'd come to know as his best friends. Out in the desert, he could faintly see the rocky trail he'd first ridden out on, following the river.

One glance over his shoulder at the small village now hidden from sight by the juniper trees and foothills and he was on his way over the flat lands, filled with sage and cactus.

Coming down in to the valley, he'd stopped to look out and see the large estate, surrounded by trees about a half mile off. He wondered where she would be at this time in the afternoon. He smiled to himself as he kicked his horse to go faster and turned it to the lane that led down in to the seaside city. The home of the Conquistador Jorge Reñaldo sat nestled among the foothills, overlooking in to the port. He looked cautiously at the wagons and buggies driving past him, in the chance that he may see someone he knew. Passing one, large elegant carriage, he took off his hat and bowed his head to the driver.

Arman stopped by the side of the road, looking up at the gracious tree lined avenue towards the grand house, it's windows now lit up from within in the early evening light.

Getting off his horse, he walked it the rest of the way down the shaded lane. One of the hands, met him outside and speaking softly, told him the Senora was on the veranda. He thanked him, giving him a couple of silver coins out of his pocket as he took the reins from him and led his horse around to the back. Dusting off his boots, he walked quietly around the house and stopped. He caught her looking out to the bay, watching the ships that were anchored there, a wistful look on her face. He laughed to himself, humming lightly a little tune, stepping forward. She turned an amazed look on her face. Smiling, she ran to him, hugging him as called her name. They held each tenderly for a few minutes, glad to see each other again. Leading back towards the house, he told her he was there to take her with him and build a new home in the mountains.

After a quiet ceremony, in which the Conquistador quietly conceded defeat and gave away his beautiful niece to the man who would carry her away to the tallest mountains she would have ever seen and make her the happiest woman in the world. Shaking his hand, Renaldo pressed a folded pice of paper into his hand, reminding him of the agreement he had required of him before the marriage. He nodded, tears in his eyes, agreeing to what he requested. That to hold the estate intact, when and if something should happen to him. Nodding, silent, he grabbed the reins and led the fine carriage to the door to retrieve his lovely new bride. She appeared at the doorway, holding a bonnet and cloth satchel. Their boxes had carefully been packed onto the back of the carriage by the servants, who had hugged her tearfully, wishing them both well as they said their farewells.

The ride out of the small seaport led them along the ridge that looked out over the water, clear and blue as ever. She sighed, knowing she would not return to the area. Turning to her, Arman promising a wonderful future in a beautiful place far in to the northern mountains. One month later, found them standing together, watching as a steady stream of people traveling by wagon and horseback went by, on their way to the west coast, looking for gold. The Oregon Trail, it was known as, a rough trail marked by thousands of men and women who had ventured across the nation in search of a fortune. Arman, an experienced miner, had taken advantage of the many rivers and streams across the mountains of the Sierra Nevadas, plentiful in the ores and minerals so desired.. It was there, near the lake, that he had found a couple of pieces of gold, nuggets worth the effort, he had told her. They had made camp for a few days and he spent long afternoons, teaching her to how to pan for the small bright bits of rock, Arman watched as the small leather bag filled slowly with the stones that would help them build their new home. A turn down in to a pine filled canyon, led to a beautiful large lake, that went on and on for miles. They were in awe of the beauty and the peaceful surroundings. A small town had sprung up on the outskirts of the lake and they had the good fortune of meeting up with two of the best trappers in the area who asked which way they were going.

"East, towards the Rockies, my friends," he replied. "Mapped it pretty well last season."

Generously, the men offered to go along with them for while acting as guides in an unknown territory to Arman. He agreed and let them lead the way across a rough and rocky trail, filled with signs of travelers. At last, the open and dry land appeared before them that would lead to the great mountains that sat east of the lake lined with white sand, they would later find out was salt. The large lake was rimmed with the white mineral and they were excited to see in the distance the large granite mountains that would become home not far off. The guides they had met, had left them with a packet of pelts to sell and a promise to find them once again if they were in the southeast mountains. Cordero promised a good night's stay and new horse for each as he shook hands with them, thanking them for their help. Mariatta had often been found sitting working on her needlework and small drawings, which she kept in her large fabric bag., now sat judging the distance as another's few days ride. With that, they decided to cross the great valley and camp at the base of the mountains. It was here, they found the narrow rocky canyon that led to the high valleys which he had come to know through the following summer. The two fine purebred horses given to Arman by the conquistador had rivaled even his own purebred stallion tied to the back of the wagon as they made their way down in to the valley. He was sure, the rest of their travel would include narrow and winding trails that may mean leaving the loaded wagon behind. At last, a small town appeared, lights shining through the windows as the sun set over the mountains. As they passed by the first small log cabins set in to the thick trees, a man hailed them, calling out a greeting. "Good evening, sir, mam", he nodded to them. Arman stopped, holding the reins lightly as the man walked towards them. He leaned over shaking the man's hand as he introduced himself, pointing back to his cabin. After a quiet meal, enjoying the stories of their travels, the men left the two wives sitting near the fireplace as they went outside to tend to the horses. "Where did you come by such fine horses, sir? He asked Arman. "This one looks like it could be the mate to the one owned by the new rancher who lives in the south end of the valley," he said as he patted the horse on the neck. Arman replied, "This stallion was one brought over from my home in Portugal last year, sir." On that trip alone, I brought with me, a herd of twelve, two in foal." He sighed, "All sold but this one to a large estate owner on the coast." He laughed." He paid a good price, he did, but I got the best prize of all, his lovely niece as my bride." He sighed. "Mean to make our home in the valley at the base of the Cresta de la Pueda Mountains". The man nodded, then tapped him on the arm and motioned for him to come with him for a moment.

Grabbing a lantern, he led Arman down a small path to the barn where he opened the door to reveal a large covered object. Laughing lightly, he we explained that it was his job to do repairs for those that had come across the rocky trails needing new wheels made. Taking the edge of the cloth, he pulled it away revealing a fine carriage of good size, made of the finest cherry woods and leather. Arman, gasped and walked forward, running his hands down the smoothly sanded side. "This is beautifully done, sir," He asked. "Is it yours?"

"Why yes, it is, one of several I had finished last spring, this one taking the longest waiting for materials to arrive from the east." The man sighed," I thought perhaps you and your new bride might have need sometime for a fine carriage like this one," pulling the cover back over the top." "Perhaps we'll meet again once you have settled." He said/ Arman agreed and told him it would make a fine wedding present. "I will return within two weeks to retrieve the carriage, if this is enough payment for you?", he asked, holding out a small folded cloth. The man took it, unwrapping the cloth and looking inside. His eyes opened wide at the clear large green stone and several small nuggets of gold. "Yes, sir, this will do just fine, I'm sure." Shaking hands on the deal, the men walked back into the cabin and made plans for the next days departure of the Cordero's. One long afternoon, they arrived at the top of the canyon that looked into the green valley full of trees They were home, at last. As the snow began to fall that winter, the Cordero's welcomed the visits of others who would make their home in the high mountain valley. Together they would form a tight knit group of hardy people that would endure over the next twenty years as some of the first settler's in the western mountains. Hidden away were the treasures along with the stories until one day, word from family finally arrived. Joachim Cordero, his own nephew along with Jean would be arriving soon.

CHAPTER 11

Late afternoon, near a large river, appropriately called the Arroyo Pintado, which flowed down from the high northern valley, as one of the largest rivers in the area. The men arrived on horseback at the ranch of the Quinn Whitaker, just a few miles from the settlement. Discouraged, they had been sent out to find the rest of the lost horse herd.

"Wait, Josiah, you can't cross here, son", he shouted. "Come, cross here..." pointing farther down the river. "Hayah! Hayah!", He yelled as he kicked his horse into a gallop.

Catching up with him, Josiah yelled out, "The tracks lead down this side, Whit." He nodded to him as he walked his horse out into the water, swollen from the wet season.

After searching for hours the day before, the three men who had ridden out with Whitaker to meet Joachim and Jean, who had located hoof prints on the trail they believed were from the horse herd.

The fine work of the blacksmith recognizable on at least a few of them.

"Must be three, maybe four stallions, one or two looked shoed it looks like," he said.

"They must be from the same herd." He pushed on ahead, motioning for him to come.

Above the sound of rushing water, they could hear shouting. They looked quickly at each other, acknowledging that someone may be in trouble. The falls below them on the trail, dropped a steep two steps down large granite rocks, almost hidden by the thick pines. Shouting above the noise, Whit gestured to Josiah to ride back down along the river's edge and he would follow him. He had almost reached the bottom of the trail, when he thought he heard something. Turning back, he yelled to Josiah to stop. Listening they could hear a man shouting for help.

62

Racing at full gallop down the river's edge, the men dodged the pines and brush to come up short on the steep drop-off of the falls. Looking down below, they could see the tangled debris of a large log jam blocking the river. Hearing shouting from below, the looked over the edge to see a man who clinging tenaciously to the debris, fighting to hold on against the flow of the fast moving river. Josiah yelled at him as he rode down the trail to hold on, whit racing after him. They looked up as another man from the other side yelled to them. "Can't reach him, I can't reach him from here." He dropped to his knees, yelling" Can you help?" He yelled. They gestured for him to stay where he was as they gathered a rope from the horse, tying it into the saddle horn of Whit's horse. Taking the end of it, Jean waded into the river, surprised at fast the current was. The tired man, looked up, holding tightly to the log that ad been caught in the mass of sticks and twigs. Up to his chest now, Jean struggled against the flow as he reached out to him, holding the rope in one hand. Grasping onto the man's shoulders, he motioned to hold onto the rope as he tied it tightly around his waist. Clutching the debris as Whitaker started to pull the man towards the side, he slipped, going headfirst into the water. Whitaker pulled his horse backwards, dragging the weight of the man towards the banks of the river. Jean watched, cautiously making his way back towards them, a few yards away. Suddenly, a log broke free, narrowly missing him. He yelled and made a grab for a branch sticking out of the river bank. The rope lands near him, splashing water on his face. He made a grab for it, but could reach it as the river's current carried him farther down the banks towards the falls. Gathering it up again, Whitaker threw it out to him once again, coming close. He grabbed it as the main mass of branches and sticks broke loose.

Logs began breaking loose as the man struggled to catch the rope. Seeing it was impossible to get it to him, Jean, grabbed the end and dashed into the water, using his arms to reach out to the desperate man. Just then, a log came loose, floating swiftly towards them, along with other debris. They watched as it drifted towards them and then crashed into the thick pile of sticks and twigs. The log, with it's weight, broke the jam loose and it goes over the edge of the falls which were a few yards away. Clutching at each other, they watch as it went over the falls, crashing to the bottom.

Whitaker yelled out to them, to hold on and began pulling the men forward. Jean had let just long enough to secure the rope around the man, then grabbing onto a log, he waited while Whitaker pulled hard, slowly bringing him to the shore. Josiah, gasping with effort, started forward once more, swimming against the hard current. Just a few feet from the river bank, he made a grab for the brush and branches, but could hold on. The current carried him quickly towards the log jam. Thinking quickly, Isaac grabbed a long, stout stick, holding it out as far he can reach from just beyond. Jean reached for it. Seeing how tired he is, Josiah started in after Jean to help grab him, as suddenly a large swell of water caught him and carried him up and over the logs and debris. Jean yelled at him to hold on, diving for him. The logs breaking apart, as Isaac was carried over the falls. All is silent, nothing but the sound of rushing water. A few minutes go by. The exhausted men stared in disbelief, stunned. Making their way over to the side, they stood shaking.

The other rider yells from the other side to them. "I'll ride down, maybe I can reach him." He jumped quickly on his horse and started to ride down the steep slope by the river, dodging trees and brush trying to see where he had gone. Jean grabbed a coat and threw over the rescued man for warmth. All of a sudden... a hand appeared near the edge of the falls, grasping onto a large branch that had hung out over the water. Grasping it, Isaac had managed to hold on barely, as he was carried over the falls. Dangling, he pulled himself up, hand over hand. Jean sees him and began racing down the river bank, wading out to him, finally grasping his arm, pulls him to the shore. a narrow escape once more, leaving the group exhausted and grateful. They decide to return home the fastest route possible, bringing the two men with them. Shouting directions to the rider on the other side, to join them at the nearest possible crossing, they ride up and over the top of the canyon.

CHAPTER 12

The Cordero ranch, a few months later, had grown from two to five well built cabins surrounded by fields lined with log fences for the cattle to graze in. Each one had been built by his ranch hands, after being given their own piece of property. Whitaker's ranch in the south end of the valley had become the stopping place for anyone traveling from the east wishing to purchase livestock and horses. Already the biggest cattle rancher in the territory, Whitaker had hired several experienced hands, along with two or three of the settler's they had met on the way. One was the young man, Isaac, who along with his father, Marcellus had become known for their fine craftsmanship.

A delivery from home brings some of the Cordero family's belongings to the ranch. Joachim was found sitting quietly, as he looked through the items that had arrived just the day before. Noticing a large wooden that bore the initials of his grandfather, he began pulling everything out, finding some fine clothing, books and household items.

He started to put it all away again, when a second glance made him stop. He stared at the box for a few minutes and then bent down, tapping the bottom. A false bottom? He looked, puzzled, then reached for a pocket knife from the desk drawer, then began prying away the wood. He could see a wrapped bundle inside about the same size of the box. Excited, he pulled it out and unwrapped the pice of fabric that had kept it clean for many years, he gathered. It was a small oil painting. He pulled the painting out and looked at it for a long time, thinking of how beautiful the mellow colors were depicting a scene of mountains and trees, much like the ones on the ranch. Sentimental reason, he thought, must have been the reason for keeping it hidden. Putting it aside for a moment, he looked through the rest of the trunks, finding some things his wife would enjoy, handed down to them both from his mother,

Inside one old metal box, were some silver coins from Portugal and some linens, pressed neatly and wrapped in tissues paper. Finally, he sees the large, leather book that had sat on his grandfather's desk, in which he kept record of his purchases and travels. Glancing through it, a notation caught his eye. A trip abroad, indicating travel through the trade routes throughout Europe. It was a lengthy, elegant paragraph or two and he sat down with at thud, thinking of how large an estate had been left behind with two elderly cousins and one dear old caretaker of his grandfathers. It had been their wish to make sure all the family heirlooms from Italy had made it safely to Joachim and his family, with the rest going to the estate in Portugal, where his father Diego and his mother had lived for many years. Carefully making notes on a piece of paper, he wrote down some of the important items and dates to be discusses with Jean when he arrived. A smile came across his face as he turned the page there it was, the same symbol and notation, dated a month later by Antone Mercado Cordero showing a letter had arrived form his brother, Arman Ortero Cordero. The acknowledgement was of the finding of the exact location of a large gold and silver deposit high in the mountains. And with it, a legend as to how to locate it, by the stand of trees. It simply said; the element is gold, as symbol known as AU shown in his grandfather's neat handwriting, And to the side, a simple drawing of the seven trees. Thinking back, for many hundreds of years, the family estates in Italy and Portugal had been the home of fine paintings, tapestries and furnishings. The land had held a fine house with many surrounding buildings sat on acres of well kept grounds, housing staff, as well as the purebred horses and cattle. Antone had built the main house of rock, which could be seen from a distance overlooking the coast below. Joachim paused, looking at the stack of books, papers and a rolled tube of maps left on the desk

"Joachim, are you ready?" a voice asked. He looked up and saw one of his hands waiting for him. Nodding, he closed the door and grabbed his hat, putting it on.

"Yes, I need to speak with Mr. Cavanaugh about some supplies." He paused, noting the time, "Let us go now." Later that evening, the busy street was coated with a light dusting of snow. Full of people bundled up against the cold, carriages made their way to their homes. The smell of smoke from the fireplaces was heavy in the cold crisp air.

Cavanagh sighed heavily, as he turned from the front parlor window, after watching passers by on their way home. It had been a wonderful dinner, visiting with the Cordero's, and some of the neighbors. The house quiet now, except for the crackling of the wood in the fireplace. His wife had retired for the night, kissing him gently on the cheek. She knew he was waiting for Josiah to arrive and had been worried about the delay.

Josiah's family had returned to the east for the summer months and they were expected to arrive and settle in for the winter in the high valley. He dozed, lightly, eyes closed, warmed by the fire. An trip up the canyon, just the other day boasted a large fresh fir tree waiting in the corner to be gaily decorated by his wife and family for the Christmas season.

Knock, knock, knock. It was a man yelling at the door. It was Marcellus calling out to him. He jumped, hearing his deep voice. Running to the door, he flung it open. Eyes wide, he heaved a sigh, "Sir, Mr. Cavanaugh, we need your help." He paused, kicking the snow off his boots. "Oh? What is it?, He asked, ushering him in. "Come in at once, Marcellus." They spoke quietly, while Cavanaugh put on his winter gear and walked out with him to saddle up a horse. Going house to house, they gathered up a few men letting them know of their need.

Early morning came, with peals of bells that rang out through the cold air. Snow had fallen heavily during the night, leaving the ground soft and white. It was almost Christmas, preparations were seen everywhere, wreaths on the doors. An unexpected snowfall had left a foot or more on the ground, making it treacherous to travel. For those that lived in the high valley, winters often kept them from traveling down into the city for months at a time. Marcellus and his small family had settle don a piece of property and just outside the mouth of the canyon.

His job had been to tend to the horse herd, carefully brought back by the men out of the southwest deserts. A mix of purebred Andalusian and wild mustangs, they were the rare and valued horses sought after by many who traveled into the valley. The horse herd had been brought down from the high pastures before the last cold spell and had been in the care o Marcellus and Isaac Now, afraid, the men rode quietly, surveying the damage from the large snow slide that had occurred in the canyon. Fearing the worst, the men were concerned that the Cordero's and some of the hands may have been caught in the slide just after they had left that evening from the Cavanaugh's home.

A thick coat of snow had covered the dirt road along the way covering the trees and fields. They stopped, looking up at the entrance to the canyon now covered with ice, rock and snow, blocking the way up the narrow canyon. Within the hour, several men from the area had gathered at the Cavanaugh's home. Gathering gear together, they quickly rode to the entrance, wagons full of shovels and pick axes. Men arrived on horseback to begin clearing the way.

"Take this side, gentlemen and dig as fast as you can", suggested Marcellus. "I'll take this group and we'll do the same here." The men started digging through the snow, until finally winded, they rested. After a few hours, a quick meal was handed out and they ate gratefully. Progress was slow and the men were concerned. Calling out, they listened. Not a sound could be heard. Wondering, they estimated the time for the groups to have traveled through the area and did at once, jump up again, grabbing their shovels, concerned for their safety. Early in the evening, the exhausted people made their way back to town, leaving an indentation, big enough to ride a horse through, about fifty feet. A couple of the men offered to stay through the evening and keep watch, with all promising to return the next day. With the morning bells pealing, the town slowly comes to life again. A few inches had fallen and tracks from the horses and wagon were already visible, as men and women gathered for a quick meeting before riding towards the entrance. A small group of men had already arrived, when Isaac and his father brought their wagon load of gear and food.

By late afternoon, they had made a tunnel almost all the way through and around the bend of the river, hearing it rushing by under the ice and snow.

In good cheer at their progress, sure of success, the men worked on, grateful for the sun shining brightly. One after another, the men followed each other into the snow tunnel, bringing back out buckets of snow, until finally too tired to continue, they sat on the ground, talking quietly. Not quite through the other side, they had not seen any sign of the families that had traveled through that very canyon the evening before. Clutching warm tins of hot milk, they drank and ate biscuits that had been brought out to them by the some of the wives and children from town. A shout rang out, and a man came stumbling out of the opening. Part of the tunnel had collapsed from inside, about halfway through and the snow was quickly piling up. He fell to his knees, gasping. The men quickly grabbed their gear and rushed to see what could be salvaged. Working as fast as they could, they shoveled snow and ice out of the way for a few hours, until needing rest, they stopped.

Bundled up against the cold, Marcellus and his wife arrived with fresh food and lanterns. The men and women gathering by the fires that had been built, eating and talking. Marcellus began a song, singing quietly at first, then loudly, as the others joined him. They sang several verses of their favorite hymns, then with bowed heads offered a prayer for the safety of the thirty five people who lived in the high valley above. They stood silent, watching the light snow falling, tears in their eyes. Throughout the long cold night, a few of the men who had stayed nearby kept watch. One by one, the families's made their way back home. A day later, after digging most of the morning, the men break through and see sunshine. Quickly, they removed the rocks and debris in the way and a man passed through riding his horse. A sigh of relief escapes him as he saw smoke curling up over the trees ahead. He rode quickly towards the Cordero's ranch, shouting back to the others. A narrow escape had almost cost them their lives, as Joachim tells the rider of what has happened on their end. Calling out to those following, to come. Making sure the way was clear, they gathered talking as they are told of the incredible story that had happened to Jean, Josiah and Joachim.

Marcellus himself had wondered at the sight just the day before, wondering how it could be. He'd mentioned it to his wife and family as they had ridden towards the canyon entrance to be with the others. Looking up over he mountain, they noticed how beautiful it looked with the sun setting, casting a soft glow. "A sign", he'd said, "Everything will be all right, dear", he hugged his wife to him, pointing to the clouds in the shape of an angel. Joachim had rushed to the aid of the rider's behind him that evening on their way home up the canyon. As he did, he heard the deep rumble above them begin and before he could even yell out a warning, the snow had came crashing down on top of them. Big, billowing clouds of snow, ice and debris landed all over the road in front and behind them. Covering he and his wife's heads, he managed to keep them going forward down the road. They had stopped, free of the slide, as it still kept tumbling over the side of the mountain in huge waves of snow.

Shouting back, to the two wagons behind them, they could see one had made it through safely and was rushing towards them, containing one of his hands and member of his family. The second wagon, did not make it and was lost in the deep snow, now covering the road behind them. Jumping out of their wagons, the men had raced back to the spot where they had just come through. Crying softly, his wife and he had sat n the wagon watching as some of the men gathered together and began shoveling fifty feet of snow out of the way. Finally, seeing the wagon covered with snow and debris, they dug it out as quickly as they could. The horse had sidestepped out of the way and was led out of a small pocket, safe and not injured. An injured man, lay across the seat, buried by the weight of the snow. Reaching him, Joachim could see he was breathing. He and the others carried out to the waiting wagon, bundling him up against the cold. The next morning, looking out over the damage done, he knew there may have been more losses and felt immediately grateful. Looking up, he called attention The sun was shining as the families's met to talked of the incident. The man who had been injured, had slept deeply, but was not doing well. They considered trying to ride through the canyon to fetch the doctor. Jean saddled up his horse, intending to ride as fast as possible through the passage for help.

Snow flurries surrounded around him as he approached the buildup of heavy snow and he stopped, looking up. He had heard voices, he'd thought as he rode cautiously up a small incline. Coming out on top of the snowbank, he could see the canyon had been covered by a couple of hundred feet of snow. Sighing, a big sigh, he got off his horse and led it carefully around the debris, clinging to the sides of the granite walled canyon. Weary, he stopped, as it had grown late in the afternoon. Discouraged, he knelt down and prayed. With the last rays of the sun setting, sending the canyon into shadow, he curled up against a large boulder, knowing he could make it around the bend in the morning. Blinking, his eyes, from tiredness, he thought he heard voices. It was the sounds of singing, a man's deep baritone echoing through the canyon. Tears fell down his face as he listened to the beautiful song being sung, less than a half mile away he judged. Night fell, and he slept at peace. A rider had reached the rest through the tunnel, pounding furiously at the door, asking if everyone was all right. Quickly, telling the man what had happened, they went in search of Jean. He, making his way out over the top of the ridge dropping down the side into the hillsides above town. There, he stopped, early morning watching the still and peaceful valley begin to come alive with smoke coming from the fireplaces in town. At last, he made his way to the Cavanaugh home where he was ushered in and given food and drink and told to rest. Together, he and Cavanaugh went to fetch the only Doctor in the small settlement. A couple of hours later, found them at the home of Joachim and his wife, helping tend to the needs of the young man who had been injured, Miraculously, prayers had been answered and all were safe.

CHAPTER 13

Spring came, the men having forged deep and abiding friendships with each other, had worked together to build homes, raise crops and livestock. One afternoon, Marcellus rode out to see Ian Cavanaugh. Haling him a she rode up, Cavanaugh shouted, "What is son?" He paused. "what did you need to see me about?". Catching his breath, Marcellus sighed,

"I found something under the wood pile by the entrance to the mine," he said. "Whitaker had sent me up a few months agon to make sure it was closed up tight for the winter and I had built a rough covering for the opening and left it secure." He looked at him, shaking his head. "I was up there yesterday and a couple of boxes that must have been there for some time, sir." He paused. "I think they must have come from Arman himself, probably having brought them out many years ago." Nodding at him, he called to his wife to bring the man some refreshment.

"Let's see what it is you've found", he gestured to the wagon. "I'll help you bring them in." He paused. "You know the Cordero's were just here for the evening, they'll be sad they missed you." Grasping the rope handles on the boxes, they carefully lifted them out of the wagon and into the house. Kneeling by the boxes, they lifted tops of after prying open them open. "Well, let' see what have here," Ian said quietly. Pulling out a piece of heavy fabric the lay tucked around a large object, he suddenly gasped and fell back on his legs. Underneath, the dirty, rugged material they see the bright glint of shining metal.

Hurrying, they pried open the top of the other box and found one exactly the same, hidden away in the fabric. Seated by the fireplace, they pulled the wrapping completely off and lifted the metal objects out, laying them carefully on the floor. They looked just like the one's found at the falls and the one from the San de Miquel Arch.

"Cavanaugh, I heard what I heard... and I saw what I saw... and let no man ever take this away from me... it's mine, Sir, I know it to be true, God rest my soul," Marcellus stuttered. "What was it? ", He looked over at him. "Pray tell me, what happened?"

Marcellus sighed. "That old man, I swear he was there." Right above my head, I swear I thought I heard music, sounded like angels.... he must have been watching over me, sir."

"Yes, I know that to be true," he said with tears in his eyes. For many years, the Cordero's had kept these valuable shields safe., Joachim will be so glad to know they have been found, at last." He paused. "Go, and send word out to them and we will meet again soon", he said, walking him to the door. "Fetch Josiah for me as well when you get back, and tell him I'll pay him a half day's wages on top of his usual for something I need done as soon as possible.

Shaking his hand, he led him to the door, vowing to keep a silent vigil. He reached over and blew out the lantern. A couple of days later, Whitaker on the way to the corral, looked up and saw Joachim approaching with his horse and buggy. He waved a hello to him, motioning for to come inside. "Be seated", he said, gesturing to the chair. "How have you been?", he asked. Santiago nodded, taking off his hat, "Well, thank you, listen, Whit, I've come to tell you about something that has happened". Whitaker, looked at his longtime friend and partner, sensing the seriousness of the moment. He sat, giving a quiet call out to his wife to bring some refreshment for them both.

Folding his arms over the table, he began. It had started the evening after the last shipment had arrived from the Platte. He had gone through everything pretty well, satisfied that all was as it should be. But, still something told him that something was up. Riding into his homestead, his thoughts had been on making it secure for the winter, after He and his wife, had decided to stay on the Whitaker ranch to be close to relatives and friends. His ranch hands had been instructed to put the stock out to graze and remain close by as needed to feed and care for them. Their own homes ready for the long winter.

Silence, all was very quiet. Taking the fence line, he rode around his property, stopping now and then to look out over the fields and the livestock. It was late afternoon when he reached the trees by his home.

Thud... thud... thud... the sound of hoofs on hard dirt caught his attention and he looked up, catching a glance of a horse through the trees ahead. He stopped, thinking it may have be one of his own that had gotten loose, he followed. Now upon seeing it in full daylight, he was surprised. It had the beautiful lines of a purebred, a stallion, young and full of energy.

He walked up closer, quietly watching. The horse seeing the rider, started, running through the trees. Worth catching, must have been part of a wild mustang herd, he reasoned. There had been sightings of one just over in the next valley last fall. Riding towards it, he saw a glimpse of it again, trotting through the field.

"Whoa, whoa, boy:, he said softly as he got down off his horse. "Easy, now".
He walked slowly forward towards the horse, noticing how it moved. Suddenly, it reared, taking off, charging up the hill. He sighed, looking at the hill where he'd gone. Walking back, he caught sight of a movement and again he sees the stallion, crossing over the fields, this time towards his cabin. How strange, he thought. His heart raced. The stallion, a dapple grey with a long, wavy black mane, looked about five years old, he thought. The markings remarkably like the Andalusian breed that he had known from home in Portugal. A few hours later, the horse, along with the man walked down the dirt road towards his home, a bridle around the neck of one and clutching the reins of the other. Leading it to the barn, he it into a stall, closing it tightly.

He had let the ranch hands know about the find and made his plans to go out to the Whitaker's ranch to join his wife for the season. Packages and boxes were carefully loaded onto the wagon, along with some fresh game and poultry from the their provisions. He had made one trip out to the barn after another, putting away supplies and retrieving gear. Each time, stopping to look at horses he'd acquired. Pleased with the new find, admiring the broad chest, arched neck and markings. He thought he might take it for a ride before leaving. Slowly, moving towards it, he braced the stall door open with his foot, taking the bridle in his hands and pacing it over the horse's head. It was calm, content to be led out and be saddled. That's what he thought, it must have belonged to someone who had worked with it before. Wishing his nephew was there to bring it along, he mounted the horse and began a slow walk around the arena near the barn. Sensing there was nothing to fear, the horse began to run.

Horse and rider, were perfectly at ease, galloping down the dirt road at a fast pace. Finally reaching home again, he put the horse away, feeling it had been meant to be.

Onto the Whitaker ranch early the next morning, he thought. Early evening, brought another surprise as one of his hands announced a rider, coming in. Getting up from his chair, he went to the door to see a man from town standing there, a worried look on his face. Asking him in, the man nodded and accepted a drink of water, gulping it down before telling him that Cavanaugh had sent him out with a message. He had sent Josiah on an errand to the docks on the upper Colorado River, about five days ago and he had not returned. He was concerned, because the trip should have only been a few days at the most. He had been sent out to make the purchases for medicinal supplies and other goods before winter set in, giving them time to arrange delivery. Letters home to those in the east, also went with the young man, known for being an expert rider. Judging the distance in his mind, Joachim also felt he was overdue and asked what route he had taken. North, through the high mountain pass, and over, he said. He grabbed his hat and jacket, leading the man out to the barn. "Let us go, now, I know the way and we still have some light". The took off at a gallop, Joachim riding the grey stallion.

Having made good time, Josiah was just about finished with the purchases Cavanaugh had sent him to buy at the docks on the Colorado River. A few of the messages to send out to family in the east and his mission was complete. The dock had been full of people, picking up passengers and goods, as he made his way to the home of a relative of Cavanaugh's. It was here, he could find lodging for the night.

Several passengers from the last boat, had sat enjoying an evening meal together, conversing about the progress being made for those going West. Finally, turning in for the night, Josiah slept well. Morning came, finding him digging in his pockets for some coins to make a purchase of bread and meat for the three day journey home. Packing some supplies, he had purchased onto the back of his horse, he kicked it into a trot, heading towards the western mountains.

The sun had set when he at last, he stopped, looking for a place to camp for the evening. He had developed a strong sense of the wilderness, being often called upon to ride out acting as a guide at times or to go for supplies. Quite comfortable with the trail home, he made a small fire and ate some bread and meat.

Looking over his shoulder, he had the feeling he was being watched and sure enough, a short distance later, he heard distant drum beats from a neighboring tribe. He had ridden on these same trails several times before and had only seen a few out hunting, leaving him alone. Still, he held his weapon ready, not sure who was around. The trail had been clearly marked, well worn with the racks of many carts, wagons and horses that had made their way west over the last few years.

He had made plans to camp somewhere near the top of the next range the following evening, and maybe get some hunting in. He hurried to make it to the pass up ahead. A slow, low drum beat beating about a mile out. Stopping briefly to take a drink from a cold mountain stream, he thought he'd heard the sounds of hooves on the trail behind him.

It was clear he was being followed, most likely by the natives who had lived in the area for many years. Feeling no harm, but just watching him, he continued on his way. They had maintained a distance of a few hundred feet or more, when he looked up to see them riding along the ridge to his side, making him anxious. Ute, he thought, judging by the way they moved, quietly. A detour over the next ridge led him down into a valley where he found a small lake. Getting down off his horse, slowly, he looked around cautiously.

He could smell a campfire not too far off, wondering what he could give as an offering if needed. Patting a small leather pouch in his jacket pocket, he quietly walked his horse, leading it around the lake and out of the area. Ahead, just then, he saw a group camped near the river, that was a tributary to the lake. The small band of natives, looked to about twenty men, women and children. Whispering softly to his horse, he led it back down teh river bed until he felt a safe distance away.

A light snow had begun to fall in the early evening leaving a whisper of white on the ground. Knowing it was too risky to keep going the way he had planned, Josiah decided to take another route towards home. In less than an hour, he had reached the thick pines he'd come through. His horse, winded, stumbled. Stopping, he got down off it, as he wiped his face with his arm. Looking back over the trail, he walked quietly through the thick pines, leading his horse, looking for a place to spend the night. It had turned off cold, and he feared more snow. Wondering of it too risky for a fire, he gathers some twigs and sticks, making a small fire. Finally, rolling himself into his saddle blanket and tried to sleep. Already a day behind, he knew the detour would cause a delay, but sure of the route, soon fell asleep. It is quiet, nothing stirring, soft light flakes of snow had begun to fall. A day's ride still, he judged and far above the northern valley. He blew on the small fire to get it going, gnawing on a piece of jerky. A branch snapped. He jumped at the sound.

"Uh-hum, son... uh-hum", a man's deep voice said. "Whenever you're lost, call upon some help from above... it'll always be there, when you need it, son". He looked up startled, seeing an old man standing silent nearby on a large white stallion. Relieved, he stuttered, "Where did you come from, old time?" He said. "I didn't hear you ride up". The old man grins at him, "It's OK, son, I think we have met before, I just saw the smoke from your fire and thought you may be in trouble". He got down off his horse and walked over to the fire, now the only light in the deep wooded area. "Well, I sure am glad to see you, sir." He said quietly, "I wish I had something more to offer you than some jerky and day old bread, but you're welcome to join me." He nodded to the fire. "Please sit by the fire and get warm". Through the evening, they talk of the mountains, trails and hunting.

There was frost on the ground early in the morning, when Josiah awoke, shivering with cold. Squinting, he looked and saw no sign of the old miner. Feeling disappointed, he silently, he wished him a good journey home, grateful for his company the last evening. Quickly he decided to leave and be on his way. Gathering his blanket and pack, he finds a bundle on the ground. He wondered at it, obviously left by the old man. He bent over it, trying to lift it up. It is large, heavy, tied tightly shut with a rope. He sat, on the ground, picking away at the rope to open and looks inside. His eyes opened wide, seeing a portion of smooth, shiny metal. Excited, he pulls the bag aside and finds it as the other now treasured pieces of ancient armor, a beautiful silver shield. Stunned, he sat staring at it, knowing now for sure, who the old man had been. Tears filled his eyes, as he pulled it up and onto the back of his horse. Carefully, he tied it on and climbs on the horse. Grabbing his rifle, he kepi t ready as headed for home. North canyon, up ahead, he turned down into the opening noticing how the high granite walls were shadowed in the late afternoon sun. Shadows? Shadows, he thought quickly, looking up, he saw silhouetted on the high ridge above him, two men on horseback. He stopped, knowing they had seen him. He waved his hat in acknowledgement. He watched as they made their way down the slope towards him so he urges his horse into a gallop towards them. They slow, to meet up with him, as they held their rifles ready.

"Greetings!" Josiah called out. He sees the calm but serious face of Joachim and one of men from town, coming towards him. They motioned to ride... ride fast towards them.

They stopped to wait for him to catch up. Josiah raced his horse down the rocky trail as the men shouted to turn and look. He stopped, turning in his saddle, seeing natives, lining the top of the high canyon wall. He gasped, watching them. At least fifty of them, some on horseback, some on foot. Grabbing his arm, Joachim yelled at him to ride, son, ride. The natives waved their weapons in the air, yelling Ayaaaii.... ayyaaiii.. ayyaii and whooping at the men below.

A few arrows whizzed past, hitting the rocks ahead of them. The men took off at a full run through the canyon, a few short miles from the settlement.

Later, the exhausted ma n and the others gathered at the home of Captain Cavanaugh, who had just sat down to read when he heard them coming. His wife, who was busy in the small, cozy kitchen, was humming a small tune, when she looked out the window to see the Cordero's, along with Josiah, Marcellus and Isaac. She called out to her husband that they were here. Cavanaugh quickly opened the door to invite them in, saying to Josiah. "Son, son., come in." hugging him quickly. "We were getting worried for you." looking at the men attending him. "What is it, Isaac?, Marcellus?" Marcellus took a deep breath, looking at Joachim before spitting out, "It's the last one, sir... Josiah has brought the last part of the treasure home." He paused. "And what a ride, it was."

He looked sharply at the young man, asking if he was OK. He nodded and said. "Sir, I brought word of your supplies, they will be on their way in about two weeks's time." He sighed. "On the way, sir..." He paused. Seeing the tired faces, Cavanaugh asked them in to sit by the fire. "I did send word out you were late in arriving, Josiah." He sighed, heavily. "Now, what is this about an old man?" Quietly, Joachim nodded to Marcellus to go get the package. Cavanaugh, surprised, brought out his eyeglasses and putting them on.

The men, now warmed by the fire lay the package on the table, talking excitedly about the experience. Isaac undoes the rope and pulls away the fabric to reveal the large, silver shield. This one, with rounded edges, curved front and engraved symbols. Obviously, an important heirloom, different from the others. Excited, Cavanaugh looks at the men, calling his wife in to see the beautiful piece of armor. Silently, they stared at it, agreeing it also would need to be kept with the others.

That same afternoon, Gage had taken a ride out to the Whitaker ranch to speak with him about some livestock. Idly, thinking about what had led him to this part of the country from his home along the western high hills of the coast, he remembered. He had just turned seventeen on his way home from travel overseas, when a captain had acquired his services in wrangling some of the livestock and horses that had been purchased at market near the city of Puerto De La Plata.

It was there he first learned of Cibola, a legend of seven cities of gold. Tales of the cities had led many men away to the southwest and he was excited to go look for the lost treasures.. In his travels, he'd been led to meet up with the kindly Conquistador Pedro, who had paid him for his work with his horses and given him one of his best horses, along with some rare books which he had carried to a a financier. When he was finished, he had made his way inland along the coast. It was while the Conquistador Pedro and his men were at a port town, collecting on shipments of goods sold, they had been stopped on the road. Bandits had chased them for over eight miles over the rocky roads, with shots being fired back and forth. Looking out one of the side windows, the Conquistador saw four masked men gaining on them, calling out to stop the carriage.

Slowing, he orders the driver to stop. The Conquistador, refusing to get out, demanded to be let go of. Arguing, a shot was fired in the air, by one of the men. Reluctantly, he had climbed out of the carriage and stood while they ransacked the bags and boxes they had picked up at the port. Holding up their hands, Pedro and his men stood off to the side, while their team of horses were untied and led off by the bandits. The conquistador was relieved of his coins in his pocket, their weapons and the best pair of matched horses.

Amid, warning shots, they disappeared over the hill. Nodding to his men, the Conquistador had sent one of his men ahead to his home for help. Quickly, one of the hired help, comes to the house to tell Gage what had happened. The Conquistador had been robbed.

He grabbed his weapon and ran to the door. Meeting up with two of his own men, they rode quickly down the road to find them. Hearing them coming, Pedro yelled out orders to go, capture the bandits and bring back his horses. Gage, nodding to them, he and one of the men kicked their horses into a gallop taking off down the road. Moonlight, the only light, they listened carefully as they rode. Just off to the side, they heard laughter. Stopping, they creeped up on the men seated near a fire, drinking, and talking loudly.

Gage crouched low to the ground, weapon in hand, sneaking in to grab the bag that lay upon the ground, and belonging to the conquistador. Then, quietly he hid among the horses that were tied about ten yards from the fire. Reaching up, he quietly untied them, leading the two horses off, while the other man kept a gun on them. At his signal, he hit the rears of the horses with his glove, and they took off, startling the men, who jumped up, cussing loudly. Jumping onto his horse, Gage, yelled to the Pedro's man to run with the horses. At a full gallop down the rocky road, they dodged the bullets from the horseless men behind them. Winded, they made it onto the grounds, meeting the Conquistador, who awarded them both with fine horses out of his herd for the rescue. For the next four months, he stayed on to train his horses for him. Finally, preparing to leave, the Conquistador gave him one of his best stallions to take, along with a small bag of gold coins. Later, when he'd acquired his own wealth from working for ranchers along the way, he'd followed the settlers coming in from a long trip east intending to make it to the high northern mountains. It was while trapping one summer, he'd come upon the small mining town, where he found his lovely wife of the twenty years, who had heard the same story many times. Together, they had built their home in the mouth of the canyon, just ten miles from the settlement.

Looking up just then, he saw a rider coming fast towards him from town, and he slowed down to speak with him. It was Isaac, who shouted. "Gage, you are need at the Cordero's. Joachim has news for you, come quickly". Nodding, he rode with him to the ranch, where the other men, he'd come to know had been gathered.

Shaking his head, smiling at the man who had just rode up, he yelled to the others to join him as he walked across the yard and towards the barn. They followed, talking quietly out to the barn where he kept an old trunk, which he began to dig through. Kneeling, he brought out a large journal, stuffed with drawings. Joachim had tears in his eyes as he realized how the intricate and careful renderings of his nephew Jean, had came to life as piece by piece they were fit together. The pieces of paper that made up the treasure map, totalling ten in all. He read, telling the history of over four hundred years. Jean picked up the large, cream colored paper and smoothed it over the desk, spreading it for everyone to see the drawings.

Looking at it, they could see it is a detailed rendition of one of the armor found, with some handwritten notes along the bottom, telling about each piece. There, as well was the mention of the heavy breastplate found, that fit one of the valued Andalusian stallions which had been the royal sire to many of the purebreds so sought after in Europe, belonging to a knight of St. John.

CHAPTER 14

Through the long winter, Joachim and Whitaker met, talking about the best possible route to take their cattle for the spring drive to market. Taking a few of his men, Joachim set out on the trail, south from the Whitaker ranch towards the south. A few days into the drive, following the river, known as the San Juan, they walked the cattle down the river bed. Passing through the red rock canyons, they see off in the distance, one of the first symbols, drawn in the old codger's journal, which had been carefully stashed away with the others at Whitaker's place. Coming up on top of the high plateau, the men looked out over the sandstone cliffs and desert plateaus.

"Eh, Cordero... isn't this the way to the Old Spanish Trail?", Whitaker asked.
He nodded, "We should meet up with it very soon, watch for signs, we will take it east."
"Yes, sir, nodding as he rode off in the direction he'd pointed out.

He adjusted his hat, against the warm sun, leaning back in his saddle. Pulling his canteen up, he took a long drink from it. For a mile up ahead, the livestock stock drifts, all longhorns, raised by Whitaker, headed for sale. The men, drove the herd, shouting out as they rode through the cattle. As the afternoon wore on, they rode closer to the formation that Cordero had seen from a distance, a large, graceful rock arch, with another one in the distance, that could be seen behind it. They had followed the San Juan River which took them to the Southwest Colorado territory, following along the old Spanish trail. Following behind them, a team of horses pulled a wagon, which was filled with supplies and goods to be traded at the outposts. One of his men, rode back to tell him they have crossed into the trail and will follow it to the next stop.

"Let's make camp, just south of the river, tonight", he suggested to his men.
The cattle slow, as the ranch hands call out to each other to meet up.
"Come in... get some food and rest up, we have a long day tomorrow before we to market", Cordero said. The men gathered around the campfire as Cordero and Jean look quickly at the map he had folded and put inside his vest

pocket. Noted were the two symbols talked about. The way to further treasures talked about.

After the success of the drive, the families met again at the Cordero ranch, where Joachim motioned for them to join him as he walked back to the barn, ushering them in. Closing the door behind them, he pulled aside the wooden door to the cellar and climbed down, asking for them to bring a light. After several minutes, he climbed back out with a large package. Handing it out o them, he retrieved another and another, until all the packages were brought forward to join the one brought in two weeks before.

The soft light from the lanterns, shone gently over the polished metal armor, lined up against the wall, as the men with their families walked into the barn to stand, along with the Cordero's ranch hands. Greeting them, with a pleased look on his face, Joachim invited each man to take note of the details beautifully etched on the surface of each. Looking at the group standing nearby, he brought forth the folded paper and laid them out on the floor for them to look at.

Kneeling, he and Isaac lay them out on the ground, while Jean finds the careful sketch of the last one, he had done, bringing it over to them to lay beside the others. Each piece of heavy armor bearing a design that connected with the next one. Each one showing the outline of a specific area. The center one, the large golden shield from the San de Miguel Falls canyon was where the last of the treasure had laid hidden.

"Read the inscription, Whit... can you tell us what it says?", Asked Jean.
Carefully unfolding it he reads. Astonished, he hands it back to Joachim, tears in his eyes.
Neatly written on the aged paper which had been pressed inside the old leather book of Antone Cordero's was the legend itself.

The men gather, standing with their families, quietly. Joachim calls them to attention and they look up at him, waiting. He began reading and pretty soon all the pieces fit, covering years of travel and treasure hunting, with more still to come. In his deep husky voice, he begins telling the story handed down by many generations.

The day had been hot, humid and the air smelled like salt. Men, women and children had walked, for miles; they had walked up the long and dusty path, just to catch a glimpse of him. Who was he, this man, they had said, their eyes wide and wondering, curious. Just outside of the ancient city of Jerusalem, there on the hillside, surrounded by many people, sat a man many had come to see and listen to. He sat quietly speaking, searching the small gathering of people for those who may be in need of healing, which he gave humbly, at times, performing miracles for those in need, he spoke of things to come.

Suddenly, a low, murmur began among the crowd of about one hundred from the surrounding homes. From the gates of the city, several guards had come forth, walking towards the group. Intending to keep peace, they marched forward. Afraid of the soldiers, people with tears in their eyes, stepped aside to let them pass on their way up the path. A woman, dressed in long robes, dropped to her knees in front of them begging them to stop... just stop and listen, please, she begged, with tears streaming down her cheeks.

Quietly, the man stood, smiling gently at her. The story goes, That as the man walked that evening, along with a few of his loyal followers, he had asked the soldiers to join him.
They did...

The next morning, along the path, were found the seven shields, left behind by the soldiers. Handed down from one generation to another, hidden away The legacy of the Knights of St. John, keepers of the heirlooms and guardians to the man they had loved and served. The purebred stallions, a rare and powerful breed, hidden away by a Monastery and at last, the treasures collected for over four hundred years by the original members of the Cordero family, beginning with Hernando Mateo Cordero, then onto Trinidad, then to Travarres. Then passed to Antone Mercado and to Arman Ortero... and onto Diego Rafael and then to finally to Joachim and Jean Leandre Cordero, the last to inherit them.

Looking out over a large, beautiful valley, several hundred years later, one can still see the seven horsemen; Antone, Arman Joachim, Jean, Gage, Whitaker, and Marcellus, guardians, sitting on their stallions, holding their shields for all time.

THE END

Lightning Source UK Ltd.
Milton Keynes UK
UKOW04n2022160216

268514UK00002B/17/P